It was during ⬚⬚⬚⬚⬚⬚⬚
silence that f⬚⬚⬚⬚⬚⬚
*Scarlett noticed the man standing
front and center of the room,
right beside the auctioneer's
makeshift podium.*

He'd turned, and his eyes, a startling shade of
blue even from this distance, scanned the room
with an efficient ruthlessness, finding her in a split
second and pinning her down with a cobalt gaze
that could put lasers out of business. A shirt of fine
cotton skimmed shoulders of astonishing width, the
pale blue fabric providing an emphatic foil for the
deeper blue of his eyes, the sweep of male muscle
undisguised by any amount of bespoke tailoring.

Scarlett swallowed; her throat was suddenly dry.
She wondered how it had taken all of two long
minutes to register his presence. Beside him, the
rest of the room faded into a pale imitation of the
lively crowd that had surrounded her until a few
seconds ago. She chewed on her lip but could not
drag her eyes away from his.

Dear Reader,

Will has fought for most things in life, including his beloved Bellevale Wine Estate. He always gets what he wants and what he wants now is ownership of the neighboring farm, Rozendal.

Scarlett, a botanist and plant hunter, has finally found a place to call home. She intends to restore the graceful homestead of Rozendal and rewild the estate.

Has Will met his match in Scarlett, or will this be another battle he wins?

Set in the winelands of the Western Cape, South Africa, this is the story of two people, divided by differing ideologies, whose trust in love has been betrayed.

Are they destined to be kept apart by the fear of opening their hearts to one another, or will their love prove powerful enough to overcome it?

I hope you will enjoy reading their story to find the answer.

Suzanne

Heiress's Escape to South Africa

Suzanne Merchant

HARLEQUIN®

Romance™

Recycling programs
for this product may
not exist in your area.

ISBN-13: 978-1-335-59661-1

Heiress's Escape to South Africa

Copyright © 2024 by Suzanne Merchant

Harlequin Enterprises ULC
22 Adelaide St. West, 41st Floor
Toronto, Ontario M5H 4E3, Canada
www.Harlequin.com

Printed in U.S.A.

Suzanne Merchant was born and raised in South Africa. She and her husband lived and worked in Cape Town, London, Kuwait, Baghdad, Sydney and Dubai before settling in the Sussex countryside. They enjoy visits from their three grown-up children and are kept busy attempting to wrangle two spaniels, a dachshund, a parrot and a large, unruly garden under control.

Books by Suzanne Merchant

Harlequin Romance

Their Wildest Safari Dream
Off-Limits Fling with the Billionaire
Ballerina and the Greek Billionaire

Visit the Author Profile page
at Harlequin.com.

For THM—who makes the best tea.

Praise for
Suzanne Merchant

CHAPTER ONE

'No!'

Her shout should have been bold and loud, but it came out as a squeak. Scarlett's lungs burned, after fighting the overgrown driveway and her undignified scramble up the crumbling steps. The dash from Cape Town Airport, following a sat-nav which issued unlikely instructions, had been the easy part. She swiped a grazed palm over her forehead, pushing damp curls out of her eyes. Her face, she knew without the need for a mirror, would be an unattractive shade of puce, clashing furiously with her hair.

None of that mattered. She watched, mesmerised, as the auctioneer, on a stage improvised from a table—*her table*—raised his gavel. The tempo of the world had changed down. Even a clock, hidden somewhere amongst the clutter of the room, launched into its midday chimes at a painfully ponderous pace.

'Going once...' the man's voice boomed with confidence.

Scarlett inhaled a deep, shaky breath. This was her last—her *only*—chance. If she stopped this man from slamming down his gavel, her life could literally change at a stroke. She would no longer be homeless and unemployed, even if healing her broken heart would take a little longer. A lot longer.

'No!' This time she dug up every ounce of conviction, put it all into her voice, and her protest rang out across the room. 'No,' she repeated, and raised a hand, waving above the heads of would-be buyers to attract the attention of the auctioneer and make sure he both heard and saw her. 'You can't sell it.'

He lowered the gavel with what looked like exaggerated patience. He removed his glasses, folded them and placed them on the small ladies' writing desk which balanced on the table in front of him, lending him dubious authority. He scanned the gathering and Scarlett saw his eyes rove past her and then return to her face. Heads turned as people tried to identify the source of this last-minute cliff-hanger of an interruption.

'Excuse me?' The man shook his head. 'Did I hear correctly? Did you say *no*?'

Scarlett nodded vigorously. 'Yes. That is, yes, I did say no. You can't sell the house.'

He folded his arms and rested them on the desktop, shoulders hunched. A flicker of annoyance pulled at his mouth as a murmur of impatience ran through the crowd. 'Would you care then, to explain why?' The sarcasm in his tone was unmistakable. He leaned forward, surveying the upturned faces, and the backs of heads, in front of him. The show he made of looking at his wristwatch would have caused a mime artist to weep with envy and a few people chuckled.

A rush of relief made Scarlett's legs go weak. She pulled in a breath and pushed her shoulders back, bracing her knees and standing tall. 'Absolutely,' she said, making sure no wobbliness escaped into her voice. 'This house belongs to me. It is not for sale.'

A hubbub erupted. The people standing directly in front of her moved away, leaving her in a small, isolated circle. One of the women bystanders frowned, her eyes travelling from Scarlett's face to her feet and back again, and she was suddenly acutely aware of how unlikely her statement must have sounded.

She couldn't remember when she'd last slept soundly for more than a few snatched hours in a bed that wasn't a hammock in the Amazon jungle, with her knees pulled up to her chin, or a friend's lumpy sofa or an economy seat in the back row of the overnight flight from Heathrow to Cape Town. Her jeans and sweatshirt were rumpled and her hair, wild at the best of times, and now scrunched into a messy bundle at the back of her head, felt as if one of the exotic bright parrots, which swooped overhead through the rainforest, had built a nest in it. The palm of her right hand was scratched and bleeding, which meant she had probably smeared blood across her forehead.

Her teeth fastened over her bottom lip as she

kept her eyes fixed on the man at the table. He appeared to be lost for words and the small kick of satisfaction she experienced was gratifying.

It was during the charged silence which followed that Scarlett noticed the man standing front and centre of the room, right beside the auctioneer's makeshift podium.

He'd turned, and his eyes, a startling shade of blue even from this distance, scanned the room with an efficient ruthlessness, finding her in a split second and pinning her down with a cobalt gaze which could put lasers out of business. A shirt of fine cotton skimmed shoulders of astonishing width, the pale blue fabric providing an emphatic foil for the deeper blue of his eyes, the sweep of male muscle undisguised by any amount of bespoke tailoring.

Scarlett swallowed; her throat was suddenly dry. She wondered how it had taken all of two long minutes to register his presence. Beside him, the rest of the room faded into a pale imitation of the lively crowd which had surrounded her until a few seconds ago. She chewed on her lip but could not drag her eyes away from his. It felt important that she try, but he seemed to have engaged her in some sort of competition which she couldn't win. She needed him to take her seriously, not treat her like someone who'd wandered in to disrupt proceedings with a baseless claim. Fatigue and anxiety threatened to overtake her, and keeping those two enemies at bay was costing her a hefty dose of mental energy and sheer determination.

As she watched, he ran a strong-looking, long-fingered hand across the back of his neck, the spare gesture displaying a leashed frustration and annoyance. His day had been disrupted, it seemed to say, but only momentarily. He'd sweep this irritating obstruction out of his way but not without resenting the waste of his time. His hand dropped and slid into the pocket of his trousers as he rocked back on his heels. Then he threw a quiet word in the direction of the auctioneer and started towards her. The crowd parted in front of him. She could see he expected nothing less.

Scarlett's gaze was still held in the beam of his, as she watched him approach. He was taller than she'd first thought, and he towered over her own five feet ten inches. She took a step backwards, but he followed. Had he no idea about personal space? But then she recognised the move as a deliberate intimidation tactic and stood her ground. Close up, she could see that his tan was the sort acquired by long hours spent outdoors in the Cape sunshine. His dark hair, brushed back from his forehead, carried a few fine threads of silver at the sides.

To her surprise, he pulled his right hand from his pocket and extended it towards her. *Taking the enemy by surprise*, she thought, trying to kick-start her sluggish brain into action. On autopilot, she allowed him to fold her hand in his. His grip was firm and dry, and she was sure he noted her damp palm, because a fleeting look of satisfaction crossed the hard planes of his face. He raised his chin slightly and finally, *finally*, snapped the link between their eyes and swept his gaze over her. She stiffened, imagining how lacking in every respect he must find her, compared with his sleek elegance and the innate sense of power he wore like a second skin.

'Will Duvinage.' The pressure of his fingers increased slightly. 'And you are…?'

Scarlett scoured her memory but came up with nothing more than a vague stirring of recognition of the surname. Had she read it somewhere? Had Marguerite mentioned it? It was so long since she'd had a coherent conversation with her godmother that she doubted it. Marguerite's mind, clouded by advancing dementia, had, long before her death, ceased to function in any way Scarlett recognised.

'Scarlett Riley,' she said, after a pause which was slightly too long. If he thought she was reluctant to tell him her name, he was right. Something made her want to withhold her identity from him, as if by revealing it she'd be handing over a part of herself that she'd never be able to get back. Instinctively trying to compensate for this imagined loss, she withdrew her hand from his.

He shook his head. 'I'm sorry…' he glanced down at her left hand '… Miss Riley. Your name means nothing to me. It doesn't explain why you might claim to be the owner of Rozendal Manor.'

Scarlett wondered if he'd noticed the band of pale skin on the third finger of her left hand, where until recently she'd worn an engagement ring. Then she decided that nothing would escape his piercing scrutiny. She clasped her hands together, her thumb rubbing over the place where the diamond had been. She'd been surprised by Alan's choice of stone, given how passionately she felt about low-paid workers putting their lives at daily risk in mines deep underground, but he'd assured her in an offhand manner that the gem had ethical credentials. He'd looked so pained when she'd suggested he show her the certification that she'd dropped the subject. With the unimpaired clarity of hindsight, she'd wondered how honest he'd been, given the spectacular dishonesty he'd subsequently displayed.

How, she wondered, had she been so easily taken in by his smooth charm and assiduous attention? His assertion that his way was the right way, his opinion the only one worth considering. Her belief in herself crushed, she'd come out of the relationship certain of only one thing: nothing like that would ever happen to her again.

Scarlett ran the tip of her tongue over her lips. She didn't like the effect this man—Will—had on her. He made her doubt herself even more—question her reason for being here at all. He seemed ready to sweep her aside with a few words, as if she was of no consequence. She didn't know who he was, but she hoped their acquaintance would be brief. If not, his attitude would have to change.

'There is no reason at all why you should know my name, Mr Duvinage.' She articulated his name carefully, giving it the full accented benefit of her fluent French, since she assumed it was French in origin. She remembered Marguerite telling her that many of the vineyards in South Africa had been established in the seventeenth century by French Huguenots fleeing religious persecution in their home country. This man could probably trace his ancestry back to that time, as Marguerite could. She saw his flicker of acknowledgement as he narrowed his eyes, perhaps adjusting his opinion of her.

'Well, then,' he said, his voice dropping to a deeper, more intimate level, as if he wished to talk to her alone, excluding the crowd of curious onlookers around them, 'perhaps you can explain your reasoning?'

Scarlett felt as if she'd been transported back to a university tutorial, with an exacting tutor training the full force of his intelligence on her.

I think this plant is an unrecognised sub-species, because under the microscope...

The past faded away, evaporating in the heat of his focused attention.

'Marguerite du Valois, the owner of Rozendal...' She stopped. Marguerite was no longer the owner of

Rozendal. *She* was. *She*, Scarlett Riley, was now the owner—the *chatelaine*, as Marguerite would have said—of this charmed and charming old homestead. She raised her eyes from their study of Will Duvinage's highly polished leather shoes and started again. 'Marguerite du Valois, the—*former*—owner of Rozendal, was my godmother. She died recently and bequeathed ownership of the Manor to me, in her will.'

He blinked once, and the fine broadcloth of his shirt tightened across his chest and shoulders as he inhaled a deep breath. He nodded slowly.

'I see. And the terms of the will…'

'Stated that I must claim ownership, in person, by midday today.'

His eyes were hooded, but she saw the flash of a spark of triumph.

'Some, Miss Riley, might argue that you missed the deadline. The auctioneer had already accepted the winning bid. It was twelve o'clock. Another few seconds…'

'I did not miss the deadline, Mr Duvinage. The deadline would have expired at the last chime of the clock. I had at least…nine seconds…to spare.'

'Mmm.'

In that sound she heard that he'd accepted her argument. She might have won the battle, but he was obviously confident that he would win whatever war he was choosing to wage against her. He inclined his head, one corner of his straight mouth twitching with the ghost of a smile.

'Do you make a habit of living your life on the edge? Sailing so close to the wind? It must be exhausting.'

'No, I don't.' Immediately, Scarlett regretted rising to his bait. She shouldn't feel this pressing need to justify herself to this stranger. She was a scientist. A botanist, accustomed to the rigorous questioning of data, triple-checking results, leaving nothing to chance. She found her position as uncomfortable as he evidently found it amusing. 'The past few days,' she continued, deciding he did not need her to share the forensic details, 'have been unusually challenging. But I'm here, and I can provide the contact details of the lawyers in London and Cape Town, if necessary.'

'I'd be pleased to have those.' A single straight line creased the skin between his eyebrows. 'If I'd had them a couple of years ago, we might not be in this mess now.'

From his words Scarlett understood two things. Firstly, that the bid the auctioneer had accepted had come from him. She had thwarted his plans to own Rozendal. And secondly, he was not pleased about it.

'I don't know what you mean about a mess. It all seems perfectly simple to me.' She kept her voice cool. 'I'll ask the lawyers to contact you.'

'Thank you.' If ice-cold was a grade, his tone

aced it. 'Scarlett,' he added, almost as an after-thought. His eyes, unhurried, roved across her face before coming to rest on her hair. She resisted the temptation to raise a hand to check on its state. It could only be worse than she imagined.

She gave him a long look. 'My parents thought it would be amusing to have a red-haired daughter called Scarlett.'

Those eyes, lit with twin blue flames, captured hers again. 'Do they still find it amusing, now that you're grown up?'

Scarlett stared at him. 'I have no idea.'

'Ah.' One of his black brows rose. 'And how do you feel about it?'

She dug her fingernails into her palms, determined not to give him the satisfaction of a snappy reply. She'd tired of that particular joke almost before she could talk. She lifted a shoulder.

'It stopped being amusing a long time ago.'

'You could change it.'

'I could also dye my hair.'

She folded her arms and tucked her hands out of sight, in case he saw their slight tremor. She was exhausted but now she was angry too. Exactly who did he think he was?

His faint smile faded. 'Would you?'

'You have a lot of questions, Mr Duvinage. Do you always get so up close and personal with people you've only just met?'

He slid his hands back into his pockets. 'No.

But considering we'll probably be seeing each other quite frequently, it's good to get the preliminary introductions out of the way early, don't you think?'

'Are we?' Scarlett frowned. 'Why?' His supreme self-assurance set all her alarm bells clanging. She was done with men like him, who persuaded you they knew what was best, and manipulated you into doing it. Next thing you knew, you were up the Amazon looking for orchids with a diamond on your finger and a man complaining that his coffee wasn't hot enough. In the *jungle*.

He nodded. 'I think it's inevitable, Miss Riley, since we're neighbours. Welcome to the valley.'

CHAPTER TWO

THE WALK FROM Rozendal Manor back to Bellevale took Will along a well-trodden track. Although the Manor had stood empty for several years, after the latest in a series of unsatisfactory tenants had moved on, he walked this way at least once a week.

Until this afternoon, he'd used the walk as an opportunity for thinking and for planning. As the track mounted the hill behind Bellevale, curving around the shoulder of the hill which divided the two properties, he could look back at the neat, orderly rows of productive vines which covered the acres of his property.

He knew every row because he walked along them as often as possible, looking for signs of disease or stress in the ancient gnarled wood, or for how well newly planted stock was faring. The map of these fields was imprinted on his soul because nurturing Bellevale was something he'd done for most of his life. It was all he'd ever wanted to do.

But a few years ago he'd begun to wonder about Rozendal Manor. The contrast between it and his own vineyards was stark. At Rozendal, nature had taken over and imposed its own chaotic order on what had previously been acreage that produced award-winning wines.

Dimly, he remembered the time during his childhood when the gardens surrounding the old Manor had been famous too. Befitting its name, the rose garden had been world-renowned. Looking down from his vantage point on the hill, it was still possible to make out the shape of it, with rusted metal arbours at the corners and a stone fountain, now buried under ivy and long-since dry, at the centre. Roses rambled over the house too, poking out through gaps in the thatch in places. He suspected pigeons and grey squirrels had taken up residence in the roof space.

In front of the house, the gravel turning circle sprouted a jungle of weeds and the driveway between the avenue of ancient oaks, leading to the original entrance gates, had almost vanished.

It was that way, he mused, that the woman—Scarlett—must have come. How she'd found her way to the disused drive was a mystery, but her scratched hand and the smear of blood on her temple were evidence that she had fought her way through the thickets of brambles. She must have climbed over the ancient iron gates too. Last time he'd looked, they'd been fastened with a hefty chain and a padlock solid with rust.

Had she been dropped off by a taxi? Left a hire car in the overgrown lane?

Nowadays, anyone who wanted to reach Rozendal, and few people did, used the farm entrance at the side, closer to Bellevale. As he watched, the last of the cars which had been parked in the space where the kitchen garden had been, nosed their way down the track towards the main road.

Whatever route Scarlett had taken, she was *there*. He'd left her making complicated explanations to the long-suffering auctioneer, who'd had the not inconsiderable commission for the sale snatched from beneath his nose at the last second. Will could imagine his annoyance and frustration at the turn events had taken. The small crowd who'd turned up to witness the sale, delighted, no doubt, to get a look inside the fabled Manor at last, had had more excitement than they'd ever expected. He, Will, had let it be known that if he secured ownership of the Manor he'd be selling off some of the contents this afternoon. There must have been punters in the crowd who'd had their eyes on the antique pieces of furniture, silver and porcelain. It was rumoured that the French armoire in the dining room was worth the price of an apartment on the Cape Town Waterfront in the right sale.

He hoped the auctioneer had an endless supply of both time and patience. Scarlett Riley had given an impression of strength and determination and he could tell she was not to be messed with. But beneath it, thinly disguised, he'd detected extreme exhaustion and a degree of desperation. Her pale complexion should have been creamy, he mused, but it was dulled by a greyish tinge, with dark shadows beneath her green eyes. The dusting of freckles across her nose stood out in startling contrast to her pallor.

But whatever irritation plagued the auctioneer, it could be nothing compared with his own. The initial flare of fury which had engulfed him when he realised he'd lost the opportunity to own the Manor had settled into a slow-burning annoyance. He wanted Rozendal, and usually he got what he wanted.

He'd had to fight for almost everything he'd wanted in life, and he was used to winning those fights. If someone had asked him what losing felt like, he'd have said he didn't know.

For once, it had seemed as if he was going to get the thing he wanted without a battle. It was obvious that the Manor should be a part of his estate. Who else would be prepared to spend the money needed to bring it back to productive order? Nobody was as fit for the task as he was. The house was almost uninhabitable; the vineyards were unworkable as they stood. Restoring it all would be a massive undertaking and commitment, but to him it would be worth every penny and every sweaty hour spent on it.

And he'd be restoring the boundaries to their correct configuration. Originally, Bellevale and Rozendal had been one estate.

But it seemed he was going to have to fight for it, after all. If Scarlett's claim was legitimate, she owned the property, but he had no idea what she planned to do with it. When she'd had time to have a proper look at her inheritance, she might be willing to negotiate with him on a sale. She must have a life in England to which she'd be anxious to return. Winter was approaching in the Cape, with the oak trees already showing a tinge of colour, and although it was a short season it could be brutally cold and wet here, in the shadow of the jagged mountains which stood sentinel around the valley. A few days of shivering in the damp, draughty old house with the pigeons and squirrels for company would surely make Scarlett see the wisdom of selling to him.

Will shoved his hands into his pockets and remembered that he'd left his suit jacket slung over the back of one of the antique dining chairs. He'd been anxious to get away, to begin planning his counterattack in private, and to escape the noise of the speculative voices in the saleroom.

He dipped his head and then shook back the lock of hair which flopped over his forehead. The day had begun with brilliant sunshine but a bank of cloud had rolled in from the ocean, invisible to the south but a huge influence on the climate of this southern tip of Africa. The light had dampened. He kicked moodily at a pebble and listened as it bounced down the hillside, out of earshot. He looked up to study the sky.

If it rained on her first day at Rozendal, would

that hasten Scarlett Riley's departure? And why, he wondered, did the idea of her huddling in the cold and damp bother him? Perhaps he should return to find out what her plans were. He couldn't believe she would be staying the night under that failing roof. He could advise her on accommodation in several nearby towns.

Why did he even care?

Will let out a long breath of frustration and launched himself at the final incline, up the track. From the top, he could look down over his own vineyards. The sight always brought him a sense of peace and immense satisfaction. In time, he'd be able to survey Rozendal Manor and farm in the same way and experience the same deep sense of achievement.

It was just going to take a little longer than he'd thought.

As he descended the hill towards his home he reflected that Bellevale, from any angle, was the perfect example of the Cape Dutch style of architecture. His ancestors had arrived at the Cape from France in the sixteen-hundreds and quickly discovered that the geological composition of the rugged mountains in the area provided exceptional soil conditions for the cultivation of vines.

There had been a Duvinage farming these acres ever since. Their wines were famous, award-winning and deeply respected and that was not going to change under his stewardship. Sure, he'd moved with the times, now producing a percentage of organic wines, as the market demanded. He'd diversified, opening a restaurant which attracted diners from around the world, and establishing a vegetable garden to supply the kitchens. But the principles of the business were unchanged. Attention to detail, a willingness to be flexible and, above all, a deep love of the very soil in which the vines grew remained his mantra. And his obsessive belief that second best was never good enough.

The estate of Bellevale had been his first love. To date, nothing else had come close to challenging it.

He stopped for a moment, surveying the view which gave him such pleasure. The gables of the house were satisfyingly symmetrical, their sharp angles and sweeping curves pristine. The kitchen garden was at its peak, providing an abundance of fresh fruit and vegetables for the restaurant. Several cars were parked in the shade of the oaks alongside the wine-tasting facility, showing it was doing brisk business. Further away from the house, he'd had the original workers' houses converted into holiday cottages, each one decorated and furnished in understated, tasteful luxury, with its own vine-shaded terrace.

Guests from across the globe came to experience the magic of a few days spent luxuriating in the tranquillity and order of Bellevale, but he knew how hard the staff worked to achieve that ambience of effortless ease. He appreciated every single one of them, knew them all by their first names, the names of their children and their grandchildren. He'd grown up alongside some of them and never forgot that his privilege in owning the estate rather than labouring on it was simply a matter of fortune: a toss of the dice.

Now, as he approached the curved steps which led onto the wide thatched veranda, one of those colleagues was waiting to greet him. Grace's mother had worked for his parents, and they'd ensured that her only daughter received a good education. She'd known Will and his brother since they were born. She'd spooned food into their mouths as babies and later dusted them down and patted them better when they fell out of trees or off bikes. It had usually been his brother who'd needed consoling. He had always been the smaller, weaker and less determined of the two of them.

Will felt his jaw tighten, as it always did when he thought about his brother. And his brother's wife.

Grace had made the most of every opportunity which came her way, becoming a talented and well-known chef, and Will had been pleased to offer her the position of restaurant manager at Bellevale. That role had grown to include managing the holiday cottage business. Grace could anticipate problems before they arose. There was nothing she didn't know about Bellevale and sometimes Will thought there was very little she didn't know about him either.

For instance, he'd expected her to be waiting, with a chilled bottle of something fizzy, to celebrate his purchase of Rozendal, but instead she stood at the top of the steps with her arms folded and her features composed into an expression of commiseration.

'News,' she said, 'travels fast. Faster than you, it seems.' She shook her head. 'I'm sorry.'

Will frowned. 'Yeah. Thanks.'

'I put the champagne back on ice. There'll be another reason to drink it before long.'

'What did you hear?' Will reached the top of the steps and began to roll up the sleeves of his shirt.

'That some girl came running in at the last minute and claimed to be the owner who is not selling to the highest bidder. Which was you.'

Will nodded. 'It was. And it was so very nearly mine. I still can't quite believe what happened.' He shook his head.

'Is she legit? Or deluded?' Grace turned towards the double oak doors and pushed one half of them open. 'I heard she had blood on her face and twigs in her hair. Her *red* hair.'

Will paused on the threshold. The idea of this description of Scarlett Riley already circulating in the neighbourhood disturbed him. It had probably reached Cape Town already and the next thing that would happen would be reporters turning up trying to get pictures of her and a story from him.

'You heard right, but she is not deluded. Or deranged, in case anyone makes that suggestion. She is tired, but my instincts tell me that when she recovers I'll find she is fiercely intelligent.'

His words surprised him. What had made him say that? A sense of fairness, he supposed. Of being unwilling to make a judgement without a proper foundation of reason. After all, he should know how that rolled. He had a fleeting memory of the way her expression had closed down, her lids briefly shielding those green eyes, when he'd asked the question about her parents. And then there was that pale circle on her ring finger.

Grace narrowed her eyes. 'Ah. An adversary. Is there going to be a battle for Rozendal?'

He nodded and stepped into the cool, dim interior of the hall. Wide yellowwood floorboards, gleaming with the patina of centuries of polish and wear, stretched across the room, a perfect foil for the glowing colours of the Persian rugs. Copper pans shone on the walls, alongside some of his favourite old oil paintings. He breathed in the scent of beeswax and lavender from the flower arrangement on the circular table in the centre of the space and felt his energy level rise and his irritation and anger subside.

'Yes,' he said, 'there is. It'll be worth the fight.'

Grace studied him. 'Cup of tea? Coffee?'

He shook his head. 'No, thanks. But I'd kill for a cold beer. It'll help me plan my strategy.'

'Where's your jacket, Will? You were wearing it earlier.'

He shrugged. 'I left it at Rozendal. I was in a hurry to leave, but it'll be an excuse to go back to see how the new owner is getting on. Knowing the enemy is half the battle.'

He opened the fridge and pulled out a beer, cracking open the ring pull and swallowing down a mouthful before wiping the back of his hand across his mouth and pouring the rest of the amber contents of the can into the tall glass Grace held out to him.

She tipped her head towards the folder which lay on the worktop. 'There're a couple of things I need to run past you, before you start forming up your battle lines.' She flipped the file open and ran a finger down a list of items. 'The couple in Oakdean are film-makers. Apparently, they plan to scope out possible locations. How do you feel about that?'

He frowned. 'Get more details from them. It'd depend on a lot of things. Mostly on how disruptive it would be.'

Grace nodded and made a note. 'And we've had another query about a wedding…'

Will put the glass down, rested his hands on the worktop and dropped his head.

'You don't need to ask me that. You know how I feel about fancy weddings…'

She closed the file. 'Not all weddings have to be fancy.'

He shook his head. 'Anyone who wants to get married here wants a fancy wedding.' Raising his eyes and meeting her gaze, he felt the familiar flare of anger. He hated that she, and others, felt the need to treat him with compassion.

Grace sighed. 'Yeah, I know. Just thought I'd mention it in case you've changed your mind.'

'When,' he asked slowly, straightening up, 'have you ever known me to change my mind?'

CHAPTER THREE

THE WALL OF exhaustion Scarlett had hit felt as solid as if it had been built of bricks and mortar. She felt ready to drop where she stood and curl up on the floor right there and go to sleep. The idea was scarily tempting.

The auctioneer had been the last to leave. She'd done her best to explain the bizarre circumstances which had brought her to Rozendal and given him the name and contact details of the lawyers. She'd apologised profusely more than once, for the disruption she'd caused. She wasn't sure he'd accepted.

Now, alone at last, she walked out through the wide front door, her footsteps echoing in the empty hall. Two elderly armchairs stood on the shady veranda. Their fabric, once a pretty floral, was faded and stained. Some small creature, presumably a mouse, had chewed a hole in one of the cushions and helped itself to some of the horsehair stuffing.

She chose the one that looked marginally less uncomfortable and flopped onto it, toed her shoes off and tucked her feet underneath her.

The view was infinite. In front of the house the gravel drive was thick with weeds, but beyond it she could make out the beginning of the oak-lined avenue she'd fought her way up to get here. She presumed her hire car was still at the gates. It looked as if no other vehicle had used the track for months so she hoped her suitcase and back-pack would be safe in it overnight. She had barely enough energy to think, let alone find her way back to the car. And if she did, she'd have to climb those gates again, and she'd never be able to haul her luggage over them.

She'd deal with it tomorrow. What difference would one more night in the clothes she was wearing make?

Beyond the tangle of the overgrown garden, the valley rolled away into the distance. Layer upon layer of rounded hills shimmered in the afternoon sun, the regimented stripes of vines marching over them. She liked the feeling of orderly permanence they gave to the landscape. Compared with the chaos of her recent past, this slice of life, with its atmosphere of timeless peace, felt like a corner of heaven.

The vine-clad hills reached up to the slopes of the mountains which enclosed the valley on three sides. Saw-toothed ridges, like the humped back of a dragon, pierced the blue sky on one side and on another sheer cliffs of rock fell hundreds of feet, to disappear into the scrubby bush at their feet.

Scarlett felt safe—cocooned in her chair, on her own veranda, on her own land. It was a luxury she would like to dwell on and savour, if only she could stay awake.

When she woke several hours later, it was because she was chilled and damp. Darkness was creeping up the valley towards her, although the tops of the mountains were still bathed in a golden evening light. The blue sky had faded to a deep mauve and the first stars glimmered through the dusk. A bank of cloud had built up in the south. Down the valley a curl of woodsmoke rose into the evening air and a dog barked in the distance.

Scarlett pulled herself out of the chair, which seemed to have sprouted lumps while she'd been asleep, and made her way indoors. Little light now penetrated the dust-coated sash windows and the interior of the house was dim. The spacious hall, where the ill-fated auction had been held, looked forlorn, with the small desk perched on a table at the end and a few chairs scattered across the floor. Slung over the back of one of them was a dark suit jacket. She ran her fingers over the fine wool of the wide shoulders and remembered Will Duvinage standing in front of her, his hands thrust into the pockets of his trousers, his shoulders thrown back. She decided the jacket belonged to him.

She wondered if he'd return to collect it or if he'd send someone else. The prospect of seeing him again made her feel uneasy and a little twist of tension tightened around her insides. She shook her head, irritated at her response. She'd talked to him for all of two minutes and in that time had decided he was demanding and over-confident. He seemed like a man perfectly happy to demand the impossible and happy to take it as his due when the impossible was delivered. But, after Alan, she doubted there was a man anywhere whose bad behaviour could surprise her.

Will Duvinage had said they were neighbours, and she wondered exactly what that meant. Here, at the foot of Africa, neighbours could mean driving thirty miles to borrow a cup of sugar. Picking her way across the dusty floor, she rubbed at the grime on one of the windowpanes and peered out into the deepening dusk. There were no friendly nearby lights.

The silence was absolute.

She felt a stab of anxiety. She was used to isolation. Her plant-hunting expeditions had taken her to some of the most remote places on earth, but she'd never been alone. She'd always had the company of other like-minded scientists and the trips had operated to a planned schedule, with every detail thought out beforehand. Things did not go wrong.

Things did not go wrong, until they did. And on the last trip they had gone wrong in a most spectacular way.

The darkness in the room had thickened. With faint hope, she flicked a brass switch near the door and a bulb in one of the old brass wall sconces glowed into life, the light feeble behind a dirty frosted glass shade. Relief loosened the band of panic which had begun to tighten around her lungs, and she breathed more easily.

The antiquated kitchen was at the back of the house and the route to it took her through high-ceilinged rooms with ceiling fans festooned with cobwebs. Stern portraits glared at her through the gloom, and furniture crouched beneath the shrouds of dustsheets. Tomorrow, she thought. She'd deal with all of this tomorrow, when she'd slept, washed and eaten a decent meal.

A loud groan emitted from the ancient brass taps over the stone kitchen sink when she twisted one of them, using both hands to break the seal of rust which held them fast. The pipes gurgled ominously but then a trickle of dirty water splashed from the spout. Light and water, she thought. What more could I want?

A pang of hunger made her realise that what she wanted was food and she would probably not get anything to eat until the morning, when she'd have to retrieve her luggage, make herself presentable and find the nearest town or village. On her mad dash from Cape Town Airport, determined to beat the auction deadline, she hadn't given a thought to stopping for food. There was a bottle of water in her handbag and the little packet of biscuits and plastic-looking cheese from the airline dinner the night before. She'd have to make do with those. In the unlikely event that there was any food in this time capsule of a kitchen, she'd be willing to bet it would not be edible.

The exhaustion that had stalked her all day, and which had been only partly alleviated by her nap in the lumpy chair, hit her again. She returned to the hall, from where a grand staircase curved upwards to the first floor, and began to climb it in search of a bed.

She paused on the landing as light flickered across the night sky beyond the tall window. A few seconds later a distant rumble of thunder rolled over the mountains. What luxury, she thought, to be in a proper house, under a real roof, in a thunderstorm. The rainforest canopy had provided scant protection for her hammock in the jungle, and she'd frequently been soaked to the skin.

Pushing open a door, Scarlett found a bathroom with a huge pink bath and plumbing which looked as if it could drive a steam train. The next door revealed a bedroom with a brass bedstead, bare mattress and pillows and a thin rug folded at its foot.

No bed had ever looked more inviting. Scarlett crawled onto it and pulled the rug up around her shoulders. Lightning illuminated the room and thunder echoed around the valley. As her eyes grew heavy, she heard the muted sound of the first fat raindrops hitting the thatch.

When she jerked awake it was because something had disturbed her. The storm was growing in intensity, but she knew it wasn't that. Storms had never bothered her. It was something much more sinister. She heard a thump, somewhere in the room, and reached for her phone. Then she remembered her bag, containing the airline snack and her phone, was downstairs. As she fumbled along the wall, looking for the light switch, a draught of air lifted her hair and something furry brushed across her face.

She found the door before she found the light switch and dragged it open, flinging herself into the dark passage outside, panic gripping her. Whatever it was seemed to be following her, because she felt it brush against her again and she put her arms across her face, stumbling to where she thought she'd find the stairs.

As she reached the landing, she remembered seeing a light switch next to the window. Her trembling fingers located it and faint light from a weak bulb high up on the ceiling lit the stairwell. A dark shape swooped in the shadows above her.

Her only thought was to escape the furry brush of wings and the unpredictable, jerky loops of the shadow. But as her feet hit the hall floor there was a blinding flash of lightning and an ear-shattering crack of thunder and the faint light high above the stairs flickered and went out. A loud banging came from the direction of the kitchen as a cold draught, carrying with it the scent of rain and damp earth, gusted into the darkness.

A door or window must have been blown open in the storm and she'd have to find it and secure it. Otherwise, who knew what manner of creatures would find their way in to terrify her?

Scarlett groped her way to the kitchen. There was no welcoming flicker from the lamps when she flipped the light switch. Amidst the confusing clamour of the storm, the noise seemed to come from behind a door which she saw, for the first time, illuminated by a flash of lightning. She twisted the stiff doorknob, but it refused to budge. She gripped it with both hands, just as another flash and a roar of thunder ripped through the house. In the inky darkness she heard a sound behind her. She half turned, panic spiralling out of control.

A pair of arms, corded and hard with muscle, closed around her, trapping her arms at her sides and sweeping her feet from the floor.

She screamed, even though the small, logical part of her brain which was still functioning told her it was useless. Because nobody, apart from the assailant who held her in this iron-hard grip, would hear her.

CHAPTER FOUR

WILL SWORE.

Who knew Scarlett's bare heels, hammering against his shins, would be such effective weapons? He allowed himself a moment to be grateful that he had her arms pinned firmly to her sides, or her fists would be raining blows on him too.

A few seconds of silence followed her first scream while she struggled, but he felt her lungs expand as she drew in another breath and then a second scream, even more piercing than the first, split his eardrums.

'Let me go! Let me *go*…'

'Scarlett. Stop it. Stop fighting. It's me. Will,' he shouted, hoping she'd hear his voice through her panic. He'd acted instinctively when the flash of lightning had shown her, poised to push open the door to the cellar steps. He'd stopped her from tumbling into the void, but he might have almost scared her to death.

She didn't scream again, but she continued to struggle. He shuffled backwards in the darkness, relaxing his grip a little but with no intention of letting her go just yet.

'Put me *down*.' It sounded as if she was speaking through gritted teeth. *'Now.'*

'Not now. I need to make sure you're safe.'

'Safe? *Safe?*' He felt her twist her head against him, and a few silky strands of her hair brushed across his cheek. Her scent, floral with a hint of warm spice, wafted over him. He'd noticed it earlier and it reminded him of shady meadows on hot summer evenings. 'I won't feel safe until you've let me go and I've put some distance between us. Maybe several miles. Or at least a locked door...' She kicked again.

Will sucked in a breath, cursing inwardly. There would be bruises to show for this encounter, even though he was wearing jeans.

'Scarlett.' He tried to modulate his voice although his breathing had become erratic and, alarmingly, he was aware that it wasn't only the wild kicks to his shins causing adrenalin to surge through his body and his lungs to feel starved of oxygen. Because, irrationally, he liked the feel of Scarlett's body against his. She felt delicate but strong, and the baggy clothes she wore had disguised the surprising soft curves of the hips which he held, pressed against his own. If he dropped his head slightly, he'd probably find the smooth curve where her neck joined her shoulder and he could take a breath, inhale that scent more deeply...

What the *hell* was he thinking? He snapped his attention back to the present and the immediate problem which he held, literally, in his arms. Carefully, he relaxed his hold and allowed Scarlett to slide down his body until her feet made contact with the floor. He kept his hands closed around her upper arms to steady her and felt a tremor ripple through the muscles under his fingers.

The lights chose that moment to flicker into uncertain life.

Will took a step back. Scarlett stood with her head bent, the pale nape of her neck exposed. He wanted, very much, to place his hand there on her skin, to see if it was as petal-soft as it looked, but he dropped his arms slowly to his sides instead, watching to make sure she didn't fall over.

She raised her head, pushing the mass of her hair over her shoulder, removing the temptation of her nape.

'Are you okay?'

As she turned to face him, he caught the green flash of fire from her eyes.

'Forgive me for pointing out the obvious, but that is a silly question. A furry, flying creature was crashing into the walls of my room. It followed me in the dark. The lights went out and an intruder grabbed me from behind and...' She shook her head. 'Seriously, under the circumstances, would *you* be okay?'

Will felt the corner of his mouth twitch and he pressed his lips together to suppress a smile.

'Put like that...'

'It's not funny.'

'No. Not at all.'

'Then don't laugh at me.'

'I'm not. I'm thinking about the bruises I'm going to have on my shins. I'll have to wear jeans for a week and not go swimming. Or else I'll have to pretend I was kicked by a horse if I'm to have any hope of maintaining my credibility.'

Her eyes dropped and her gaze slid down his body to his feet and back up again.

'Oh… I'm sorry. Are you comparing me with a horse?'

'No!' He shook his head, raking his fingers through his hair. 'I'm sorry I frightened you. I…'

'You didn't frighten me. You terrified me, almost to death.'

'I didn't stop to think. It was instinctive…'

'I think your instincts need work. *Suppressing* work.'

Her breathing was less erratic, but he could still see the hollow at her throat moving in and out, pushing the ends of her collarbones against her sweatshirt. And he had to agree with her, because what his instincts were telling him to do right now was simply unacceptable.

'It wasn't…like *that*. I was trying to protect you.'

'Well, it *felt* like…*that*.' She raised a hand, which shook a little, and pushed her hair away from her forehead. 'Most people would have at least knocked first. So what,' she asked, 'were you protecting me from?'

Will huffed out a breath and pulled a hand

across his jaw. 'I'd come over because I thought you might be afraid.'

'It was after you got here that I became afraid. Except of the furry flying thing. Which I presume was a bat.'

He nodded. 'Most likely.'

'I'm used to bats flying around. Just not indoors. They're not scary in the jungle. Also, I'm tired. More like exhausted, and logical thought has become an alien concept.'

'I thought you might be afraid of the storm. The power is unreliable when there's lightning around. I didn't know if you'd have a torch…'

'I'd left my phone downstairs. There was something banging behind that door.' She tipped her head in the direction of the cellar door. 'I wanted to stop it. But you jumped me.'

'That wasn't how it was meant to feel. I'm sorry.'

'I don't know in which alternative universe it could have felt different. Why did you do it?'

'I was at the back door.' He glanced over his shoulder. 'That's what was banging in the wind. In the flash of lightning, I saw you trying to open the cellar door and I had to stop you.' He stepped around her, taking care not to touch her, and twisted the handle, pulling the door forcefully towards him. 'This is why.'

A void, dark as pitch, yawned beyond the opening. Once, a staircase had wound down to the extensive cellars below the Manor, but now the top three steps had crumbled away to nothing, and the remaining treads were rotten and unstable. Will nodded, satisfied that he'd done the right thing. Scarlett would have stepped through the door and into a black space. How long would it have been before anyone found her on the stone flags of the cellar floor?

He glanced back at her. He thought her face, already pale with exhaustion, had lost a little more colour. She raised the back of one hand to her mouth as she peered past him.

The storm was receding and a moment of quiet settled over them. Scarlett's eyes, wide green pools of shock, met his. He wasn't sure, in the unreliable light, if their shimmer was enhanced by tears or not. Then she turned away, swiping her fingers across her cheeks.

'Thank you.' Her voice was strained with fatigue. 'I'm sorry I kicked you. I would have fallen…'

Will nodded. 'Yes, I think you would have. But you're safe now. Just don't go wandering about in the dark…'

Her narrow shoulders lifted in a slight shrug. 'No, I won't. Anyway, I'm much too tired to wander anywhere else.'

For a reason which Will didn't examine, he hated the trace of defeat he heard in her voice. From what he'd seen of her so far, defeat was probably not a concept to which she gave much consideration. He moved to her side and touched her arm.

'Would you like me to take you back up to bed?' It was too late to take the words back, even as he heard how they sounded. 'That's not what I meant to say. I meant…'

The hint of a smile lifted the corners of her full mouth, showing the slight dent of a dimple in the middle of her left cheek. 'That's good, because I'm in no state to indulge in any bed-related activity, apart from sleep. But perhaps you need to work on your seduction technique, alongside taming your instincts…'

Will's hand shot out to steady her as she swayed on her feet. Then he slipped his arm around her shoulders.

'You're shaking. When did you last eat?'

'That's because of your inappropriate suggestion. And my last meal was an airline one.'

'You haven't eaten? *All day?*'

'Mmm.' She nodded. 'Intermittent fasting is supposed to be good for you.'

'Well, in your case it's going to cause you to pass out, and that will definitely not be good for you.' Will came to a snap decision. 'I'm taking you home to Bellevale. You can sleep in a clean bed and have some proper food while you decide what to do about Rozendal Manor. You'll need to be sharp to talk to the lawyers about planning and timing for the sale.' He bent and put his free arm under her knees. But then he paused. 'Scarlett, I'm going to pick you up and carry you to my four-by-four. It's parked around the back of the house. Is that okay?' Another struggle was the last thing he wanted.

'Um… I suppose so. Yes.' A yawn blurred her speech and he felt her body sag against his. As he scooped her up her head dropped to his shoulder and her hand rested on his chest. Then she raised her head slightly. 'I already know what I'm going to do about Rozendal Manor.'

'Good.' He hoped the relief didn't show too obviously in his voice. If she'd made up her mind it would all happen more quickly than he'd dared to hope earlier in the day. She had determination, he could tell, and was unlikely to change her mind. She must have seen the impossibility of doing anything with the Manor apart from selling it. And he was prepared to make her a generous offer, which she would be foolish to refuse.

'Yes,' she said, her voice soft. 'It's so beautiful here. It's as if the house and garden have been asleep, waiting for someone to wake them up.'

'Tomorrow, I'll take you in to the lawyers' offices in Cape Town, if you're ready.'

Her head dropped back onto his shoulder and he settled her into his arms.

'That's very kind of you,' she murmured, 'but not necessary. I'm not selling. I'm staying at Rozendal. I'm going to rewild the estate.'

CHAPTER FIVE

As BOMBSHELLS WENT, Scarlett's announcement was up there with the one his brother had made five years ago. After that, he'd vowed he would never be caught out by anyone, ever again.

Since that day he'd been ready for every eventuality, every possibility. Every disaster. He never wanted another surprise. He never wanted to feel that sense of confusion again, as if the person standing in front of him was speaking in a language he knew he should understand but which sounded utterly foreign.

It had felt like a nightmare from which he'd never wake up, and then it had been made worse by the real, proper nightmares that had plagued him for months. He'd woken from those, only to be hit again, each time, by the dawning of reality, the sense of humiliation and embarrassment, and the realisation that you could not trust anyone—not even the people you'd believed were closest to you.

He stumbled, and crashed into the old oak table which stood in the centre of the room. His arms tightened around Scarlett reflexively, protecting her. She didn't react and as he stood, attempting to regain his equilibrium in more ways than one, he realised, from her steady breathing, that she was asleep.

The shock he'd had this morning when she'd appeared, a dishevelled vision with twigs in her incredible hair, to snatch the ownership of Rozendal from him, had been intense. He'd been on the brink of achieving his goal but he'd kept a lid on his temper, knowing only the muscle tightening in his jaw would give it away, and he was almost sure nobody in the crowd had seen that. The rapt attention in the saleroom, which had been focused on him, had switched in an instant to Scarlett. He felt grudging gratitude for that. Some smooth lawyer in a fancy suit, sent to make the claim on her behalf, would not have generated one tenth of the interest she had.

He drew in a calming breath, telling himself that his plans for Rozendal were on hold, not cancelled. Scarlett's appearance and claim were simply a little difficulty he had to navigate, and he was used to managing difficulties. Sometimes he felt as if his whole life, until he'd locked a copy of the deeds of ownership of Bellevale in his safe, had consisted of overcoming one difficulty after another.

Except for that unpleasant business with his brother, which had come a little later.

This was just another one, sent to prove that he would always—*always*—succeed in getting what he wanted.

He carried Scarlett through the open back door and kicked it shut behind him. If there was a key, he didn't care. It had been open when he'd arrived. The stone steps down into the yard were treacherous, the rain having left them slick and slippery. When he reached the bottom, he realised he'd been holding his breath. Falling down the flight with Scarlett in his arms would have been a disastrous end to what had been a difficult day.

Scarlett stirred as he slid her onto the back seat of the Range Rover. She cupped a hand under her cheek before settling into sleep again. Will climbed into the driver's seat and took out his phone, pulling up Grace's number. She never left the restaurant until the last of the diners had taken their leave and the staff had finished clearing up, leaving the tables and kitchens pristine and gleaming, ready for the following day. She'd still be there.

'There's an unexpected late guest,' he said when she answered on the third ring. 'Is there a cottage free?' He refused to face the possibility that there might not be. Of course, he had guest bedrooms in the homestead, but he guarded his space and privacy fiercely, and sharing them with Scarlett would be an absolute last resort. In the background he could hear the sound of the kitchen being cleaned, then a door closed and the noise faded.

Grace could be counted on not to ask unnecessary questions.

'Sure,' she said calmly. 'The couple who particularly requested quiet and seclusion cancelled. One of them is ill. Which means Vineyard Cottage is free, as long as your guest doesn't mind solitude.'

'She's practically comatose at the moment, so she is not going to mind anything.'

There was the briefest of pauses before Grace replied. 'I see. Okay, I'm just finishing up here, so I'll drop by the cottage on my way home to unlock it. Do you,' she asked, and Will could hear the tact in her voice, 'need any help?'

'It's the girl from Rozendal, Scarlett Riley,' he said, deciding to short-circuit any speculation on Grace's part. 'She's exhausted, travel-stained and asleep. Definitely not a subject for you to start weaving a romance around.'

'I wouldn't dream of it.'

'Yeah. That's what you always say. I'll be there in ten minutes.'

When Scarlett eased her eyes open, the first thing she became aware of was the light. It wasn't the greenish, watery light, filtered through the jungle canopy, accompanied by the calls of unfamiliar birds and the squawks of parrots. Neither was it the soft, pale light of an English dawn in spring. It was bright and hard-edged, falling in sharp bars through the wooden shutters onto the pale timber floor. It was completely alien.

Her confusion grew as she studied the room through half-closed eyelids. Nothing about it was familiar.

The walls were painted in a chalky white and green-painted timber framed the window and doorframe. She lifted her head a little and caught a glimpse of the inside of a luxuriously appointed bathroom. With a jolt of surprise, she realised that the jeans and sweatshirt she'd been wearing—for how many days?—lay neatly folded on a low chair. Soft linen, of what felt like a zillion thread count, caressed her legs and the bed was not a hammock or a lumpy sofa, or even an airline seat. It was wide and comfortable and she wanted to stay right here, in it, for ever.

She shot upright. Where was she? And how had she got here? And, for that matter, who had removed her clothes and tucked her into this dreamy bed, leaving her in her underwear and tee shirt?

She pushed back the light-as-air duvet and swung her legs to the floor. It was when she noticed her dusty feet that the scattered pieces of the jigsaw which made up the past few days began to fall into place.

She'd taken off her trainers before climbing into that other bed: the one with the hard pillows and threadbare blanket. And she hadn't put them on again when she'd fumbled her way downstairs, a dark shadow looping above her head, there'd been a storm and the lights had gone out and...

Will. Will had scared her, but he'd stopped her from tumbling down that gaping hole, into the cellar. He'd picked her up. And after that she couldn't remember anything at all.

Had Will brought her here? Had it been Will who had removed her jeans and tucked her into bed? She lifted the hem of her tee shirt and looked at her worn old underwear and groaned in embarrassment, but she suppressed it immediately.

She didn't care if Will had seen her panties. She didn't care who saw them. She was so over worrying about stuff like that.

Standing up, testing her legs because they didn't feel as if they truly belonged to her, she walked to the window and eased back the shutters. The bright African sunlight struck her face, making her blink. From the position of the sun, she thought it must be late morning. It was a long time since she'd slept for so many uninterrupted hours. Her body felt light and energised, her brain clear. The heartache and regret which ambushed her within seconds of waking nowadays had retreated to the edge of her consciousness and she hoped she could keep them there.

Behind the full-length shutters was a pair of French windows which opened onto a deep terrace, shaded by a gnarled vine whose leaves were edged with the first golden tinge of autumn. Rows of cultivated vines divided the slopes which fell away into the valley, while beyond them the mountains etched a jagged outline against the deep blue of the sky.

The scene of orderly tranquillity settled around

Scarlett like a comfort blanket as she remembered that she was a part of it now. Okay, Rozendal was neither orderly nor tranquil yet, but she would transform it. The estate would become a haven for wildlife and rare plants, an organic oasis of productivity and creativity. Her imagination raced ahead into the future.

This timeless valley was her home, and Rozendal the only place she'd ever been able to call her own. She felt as if she belonged, even though she'd only been here for a day. She savoured the thought, scarcely daring to believe it. She, Scarlett Riley, was no longer the abandoned, homeless, botanist. She was the owner of Rozendal Manor and its glorious gardens and acres of land.

'Thank you, Marguerite,' she breathed. Her eccentric godmother had rescued her from the ignominy of having to spend the holidays at her boarding school when her hapless parents had failed to make alternative arrangements for her. She'd taken her on adventurous trips, hunting for rare plants, and on chaotic visits to the seaside and up Scottish mountains. She'd been there for all the milestones that her parents had missed. And she'd waved Scarlett off on that last fateful trip to the Amazon, in a sudden moment of clarity, as if the clouds had momentarily cleared from her foggy mind.

'Be sure that you're sure of him,' she'd said, glancing at Alan's retreating back as he'd marched out of the door of the care home, without waiting for her to follow.

And then, on a rare occasion when she'd been able to connect to the internet at some jungle outpost, she'd learned that Marguerite had died.

Alan had had little patience with her grief, uttering a few empty platitudes before tucking into his breakfast, and Marguerite's words had come back to her.

Was she sure of him? She'd realised she didn't know. And the middle of a jungle expedition was probably not the time or place to start having doubts. She'd deal with them later, when she was back on familiar territory, and when her safety didn't depend on him.

Marguerite had rescued her again, and this time it was for keeps.

Scarlett breathed in a lungful of the warm, scented air. It reminded her of golden honey trickling from a silver spoon, of the lavender cushions Marguerite had tucked under her pillow—'*French* lavender, darling, naturally. *Never* English'—and of the jasmine which had scrambled through the old apple tree in her small London garden.

'Thank you,' she said again, only this time she spoke the words out loud.

Then she noticed two things. Firstly, to her shock, Scarlett recognised her hire car, parked under the towering oak trees which shaded the cottage. And secondly, she saw her battered suitcase standing on the veranda beyond the French windows, her handbag balanced on top of it.

Fumbling with the latch, she managed to open the windows. The tiled surface was warm beneath her feet as she stepped outside to retrieve her luggage.

Then she saw something else. It was Will, and he was striding with purpose towards her. She wondered if she had time to dart back inside and close the shutters again, pretend to be asleep.

But he'd seen her, and he quickened his pace. He looked as fresh as she felt rumpled and undressed. His faded denims encased powerful thighs and she had a sudden, disturbing memory of the rock solidness of them, pressed against her, as he'd held her tightly in his arms the previous night. She pushed the memory away as Will stopped at the foot of the three steps which led up to the cottage, only to focus on the width of his shoulders and the tanned, powerful forearms which his rolled-up sleeves revealed instead.

Scarlett swallowed hard, gripped the hem of the tee shirt, pulling it down so it reached the top of her thighs, and lifted her chin. Men like him should come with a warning.

'Good morning.' His voice was dark and rich. It reminded her of strong coffee and how much she needed a cup of it right now. He glanced at the watch on his wrist, and then back up at her. 'It is still morning. Just. Which means you must have slept well?'

'I...yes. Thank you, I did. I've only just woken.'

'Good. You were practically unconscious last night. I was coming to unlock the door.' He nodded towards the front door behind her and a little to the right of where she stood. 'We locked you in last night, but I knew you could find your way out through the French windows if necessary.'

Scarlett scoured her memory but nothing—not a single detail—floated to the surface.

'We? You and...who else?' She felt a new rush of anxiety and embarrassment at the thought of some other, unknown person taking off her jeans, putting her to bed.

Will smiled, his eyes crinkling at the corners and the lines bracketing his mouth deepening. 'You needn't be embarrassed. You were very tired. Grace, who manages the restaurant and the B and B business, met us here. It was Grace who put you to bed.'

Scarlett frowned. An image of someone willowy and elegant swam across her mind's eye. Someone who worked alongside Will and who he felt comfortable about contacting late at night when he had a problem. A problem in the form of an unexpected visitor who had fallen asleep in his arms. The idea of such a person undressing her and putting her to bed did not make her feel less awkward.

Then she remembered that she was supposed not to care who saw her underwear. She released the hem of her tee shirt and stood a little taller.

'Thank you. Please thank Grace too. I'm sorry to have caused you trouble.'

Will's shoulders lifted. He shook his head. 'No trouble. I'm glad I went to check on you. You were...'

'Yes,' she interrupted. 'I remember. Thank you for stopping me from falling down those stairs too.'

The smile disappeared from Will's face. 'You can thank Grace yourself. You'll see her later.'

'Oh, no, I won't be here long. I need to get back to Rozendal. There's so much to do.'

Will mounted the steps slowly. He stood looking down at her, his hands in his pockets.

'Well, you say you don't mind the bats, so I'm sure you won't care about the squirrels and pigeons living in the attics either. And once you've worked out which boards are safe to tread on, you won't go through the floors. The rusty water—' he shrugged '—it's not drinkable, but you could wash in it, I suppose.' His eyes left her face and moved to her hair.

She chipped in before he could state the obvious. 'So the rest of me will become the same colour as my hair. That'll be interesting. And if you're trying to put me off, you're wasting your time.'

'I'm not trying to put you off. I'm hoping you'll see sense, that's all. The place is unsafe and uninhabitable. The booking for this cottage was cancelled yesterday so it's free for the next fortnight. I can't make you stay here, but you'd be crazy not to.'

His offer surprised Scarlett. After all, she'd thwarted his very nearly successful bid to buy Rozendal from under her nose. Was that only yesterday? Time seemed to have taken on a new dimension and the reality of her last-minute flight and dash from Cape Town felt as if they'd happened in another universe.

If she'd had time to consider it, she would have assumed he'd try to get her to leave as quickly as possible. He wouldn't have succeeded, of course. She'd made up her mind and she wasn't going anywhere, but he wasn't to know that.

His expression was serious as his eyes came back to her face. She looked away quickly, not wanting him to catch her studying him, and found her gaze level with the undone top button of his pastel blue shirt. The exposed vee of skin was smooth and tanned. Was he tanned like that all over? Well, not *all* over, obviously…but then, had he mentioned swimming last night?

Warmth rose in her cheeks, but if he noticed her blush he ignored it.

'I need to get dressed. Then I'll drive over to Rozendal and make a start. If you could direct me to the nearest place where I can buy bed linen, and food…' She stopped. Will's voice had made her think of coffee, but it couldn't have conjured up that tantalising aroma, could it? And layered beneath it was the scent of freshly baked pastries. Hunger, which she'd managed not to acknowledge until now, slammed into her. She resisted the urge to clutch at her stomach. 'Is that…?'

'Here's breakfast. A little late, but I'm sure you're hungry enough to forgive that.'

Beyond Will, an ebony-haired woman had appeared. She climbed the steps and placed the tray she carried on the small, round table in a shady corner under the vine. When she straightened up, she extended a hand towards Scarlett.

'Hi. We met last night, but I doubt you remember. I'm Grace. You must be starving. Enjoy your breakfast.'

Scarlett liked the warm, firm grip of her hand, and the way her smile reached her dark eyes. She was friendly and carried an air of capability.

'Thank you. And for…last night too.'

'You're welcome.' She glanced across at Will. 'I'm practised at putting people to bed. It started with Will and his brother when they were babies. Not forgetting a couple of times when they were teenagers…'

'Okay, Grace, no embarrassing childhood stories. I see there're two mugs on the tray. Is one of them for me, or are you planning on sharing Scarlett's breakfast?'

Grace shook her head. 'Much as I'd like to get to know you, Scarlett, I've got too much to do this morning to spend time drinking coffee. When I saw you chatting, I added another mug to the tray. I'll see you later.'

She left, leaping down the shallow steps and striding away, hips swaying as she pulled out her phone and made a call.

The idea that Grace had helped her to bed made Scarlett feel less uncomfortable. She longed to tuck into the coffee and pastries, but knew she had to put on something more than a tee shirt first.

'I'll get dressed...' She bent to pick up her suitcase, but Will was there before her.

He swung the suitcase up and walked into the bedroom, putting it on a luggage rack at the foot of the bed. 'You'll find a robe behind the bathroom door. Put that on and come out to eat.'

With that, he strode out of the door, his tall frame briefly blocking the light. The room dimmed as he pulled the shutters closed behind him. Seconds later, Scarlett heard him unlocking the front door. She slipped into the bathroom, splashed cold water onto her face and looked in the mirror.

Worse. Much worse than she'd imagined.

Her hair looked as if it had partied all night. She located the scrunchy she knew she'd used to tie it back. Had that been in London? Then she pulled it into an untidy knot on the top of her head. She stripped off the long-sleeved tee shirt and pulled a towelling robe from the back of the door, sliding her arms into its luxurious softness and tying the belt firmly at her waist.

As she walked back into the bedroom, she realised she'd done exactly as Will had told her.

CHAPTER SIX

THE ROBE REACHED to an inch above her knees, but as Scarlett walked towards him across the tiles he caught a glimpse of a smooth thigh as it flipped open. Her slim legs were long, her feet delicate and covered in a layer of grime. She'd pulled her hair onto the top of her head but some of it had already escaped, framing her face in russet-coloured tendrils. As she approached, she tucked them behind her ears and he noticed that her hands were delicate too, with long fingers and short nails.

The movement as she turned her head to look at the tray on the table was measured and graceful and he wondered how she could be so controlled. If he hadn't eaten for that many hours he'd have reverted to a neanderthal, with any manners forgotten.

He pulled out one of the wicker chairs for her and she sat down, her actions deliberate. But when she raised a hand towards the coffee pot it was shaking.

'Let me.' He reached out to grip the pot, his fingers brushing against hers. 'You're trembling, presumably with hunger.'

She nodded. 'Yes, I'm a bit light-headed. Now that food is within reach, I feel almost too weak to eat it.' She slumped back against the deep cushions of the chair and closed her eyes.

Will lifted the linen cloth from the basket of pastries, tore a piece off one of them and reached across the table.

'Eat this, Scarlett. But nibble it. Don't swallow it all in one go or you'll feel ill.'

She opened her mouth and he touched the flaky morsel to her lips. Then she took it from his fingers and ate a piece, swallowing slowly before taking another bite.

'Mmm.' Her eyes fluttered open. 'Delicious.'

Will smiled. 'Good. They're made in the restaurant kitchen every morning. Coffee?'

'Yes, please. I might die if I don't have coffee soon. But, on the other hand, the smell of it makes me think I've died and gone to heaven, anyway. Win-win.'

'It's good that you're feeling better.' He lifted the pot and poured steaming black coffee into the two china mugs. 'Milk? And I think you should have some sugar.' He dropped two lumps of golden-brown sugar into one of the cups.

'I don't take sugar.'

'It'll be good for your energy levels. Just this once.'

'Has anyone ever told you you're bossy?'

He shrugged. 'All the time. I'd worry if they didn't. I'd think I was losing it.'

Scarlett sighed. 'I'll listen. Just this once, then.

But no more sugar after that. However, after another couple of those pastries I'll feel fine. And I don't mean a couple of bites. I mean *whole* ones.'

He pushed the basket towards her, trying to stop his brain from wondering what she was wearing under the robe. What was *wrong* with him? He remembered, with annoyance, his slip of the previous evening, when he'd been holding her in the dark, tantalised by her scent and wondering how the skin of her shoulder would feel beneath his mouth...

A leaf from the tangled vine drifted down, one of the first casualties of the approaching change of season. It settled on her hair. Will leaned forward to brush it away but she tilted her head.

'What are you doing?' A wariness in her tone made him stop.

'There's a leaf. It's exactly the colour of your hair.'

'Red.'

'Not red. Russet.'

She patted her head and lifted the leaf between thumb and index finger, holding it up to the light. The sleeve of the robe fell back to her elbow.

'Mmm.' She released it and watched it float downwards to land on the tiles.

Then she helped herself to another pastry and his eyes fixed on her forearm. A series of deep scratches ran from her elbow almost to her wrist. They were healing but still looked angry around the edges.

Too late, he felt her eyes on him. There was no point in pretending he hadn't seen the injury. He could tell she was waiting for the question.

'What happened to your arm?'

'Oh, that.' She pushed up the other sleeve of the robe to reveal similar marks. 'I was looking for orchids.'

'Orchids?'

'Yes.' She gripped the handle of her coffee mug and raised it to her lips, taking a sip and grimacing. 'I'm sure the sugar is good for me. Just this once.'

'Presumably these elusive orchids were not in an English country garden.'

'No. No, they weren't. And, technically, I'd already found them but I'd lost them again.'

He waited for her to continue. She examined the pastry in her hand and took a bite from it.

Will was intrigued. Not just by the lack of information, but by her attitude. By *her*, he admitted with a degree of reluctance. He couldn't remember when he had last found a woman intriguing. Desirable, yes, usually for a very short time, and never by the following morning, which was why he never spent a night in a woman's bed, and never, ever invited one into his.

But intriguing? That was something different. That meant wanting to know more about her. Possibly *everything* about her. And that meant spending time getting to know her, and then she'd want to know all about him, and that was where the story would end. His life was his. Nobody else needed access to it. He had all he'd ever wanted. He had Bellevale.

But, he told himself, perhaps he needed to know something about Scarlett if he was going to persuade her to sell Rozendal to him. Which he was going to do. There was no doubt about that. If he could understand how her mind worked, which buttons to press, the whole process might be quicker. That had to be a good thing. So he asked the next question.

'Where were you hunting for orchids? Where have you been, to get injured like that?'

Scarlett swallowed another mouthful of coffee and put the mug back onto the table. She wiped crumbs from her lips and licked sugar from her fingers—an action which Will found seriously distracting—and pleated the linen napkin on her knee, pressing it down with the heel of her hand.

'The Amazon,' she said, her tone matter-of-fact, as if she'd mentioned popping down to the local flower market.

'The *Amazon*?'

'Yup.' She nodded. 'It's a rich hunting ground. Amazing flora, obviously, for a botanist.' She paused. 'But the jungle is…' she glanced down at her arms '…scratchy.'

Will thought he could come up with several other ways of describing the jungle. Dense, dangerous, scary… Scratchy was not a word he would have chosen. Rose bushes were scratchy. Or thorn trees in the bush. The Amazon rainforest demanded a whole different level of description.

He tried to reassess his opinion of Scarlett. That opinion, after all, was based only on his very brief encounter with her yesterday. She'd appeared from nowhere, seemed chaotic and lost, and her vulnerability had played on his mind enough for him to return to Rozendal last night, in the middle of the storm, to check on her.

But perhaps she wasn't vulnerable at all. She must be strong and intrepid if she'd been plant-hunting in the Amazon. She was a botanist who had the crazy idea of rewilding Rozendal. Perhaps this was going to be more difficult than he'd thought. He glanced down at her hands, but she'd folded them in her lap, on top of the napkin, her right hand over her left. Had he imagined that pale circle on her ring finger? He was sure he hadn't, but he felt wrong-footed, his judgement flawed, so perhaps he had.

'I thought,' he ventured, trying a different approach, 'that you're meant to "take nothing away, leave nothing behind".'

Scarlett rolled her shoulders and her eyes met his. He saw defensiveness flicker in their emerald depths.

'Oh, we… I wasn't taking the orchids away. I was mapping them. All I took away was a photograph. And I left nothing behind.'

He noted that little correction and mentally filed it away for another time. If he always asked the question she expected, she might think he was predictable. He needed to keep her guessing about what he was going to do.

He leaned back in his chair and stretched out his legs, crossing his ankles, trying to look relaxed and not as if he was analysing her every word and action.

'How,' he asked, 'did you get from the Amazon to here? Those scratches look quite recent.'

She went quiet as she appeared to be working something out, her brows pulled together.

'Let me see… I had two nights in London, before flying to Cape Town.' She ticked them off on her fingers. 'Then I spent about six days trying to find my way back to the camp, although it might have been longer. I lost track of time a bit. So they're just about a week old.' She eased the sleeves back down to her wrists. 'And now if I have any more pastry or sweet coffee I think I'll go into a sugar coma, so I'm going to have a shower and change and drive over to Rozendal.' She pushed her chair back. 'Thank you for breakfast.'

Will leapt to his feet. 'I don't think you should drive. Not yet.'

'Why not? I feel fine.'

He crossed his arms, keeping his hands to himself. He wanted to touch her arm, to make sure she listened to him, but he didn't think she'd like that.

'Yes, but you've been very tired. You probably haven't recovered properly yet. And anyway, I should come with you to make sure you don't fall down any steps or through any floorboards.' He tried to sound teasing, but he was aware that he was being overbearing and she might tell him to leave her alone.

The truth was he had an overwhelming need not to let her out of his sight for long. He told himself it was because he needed to keep track of her movements and ideas if he was going to gain possession of Rozendal. He refused to even begin to acknowledge the thought that it was because he wanted to be near her. He hadn't wanted to spend time—proper time—with a woman for years.

Will shoved his hands deep into his pockets and strolled to the edge of the veranda as Scarlett walked away. He was determined not to watch her, but his determination failed. He turned his head just as she turned hers, and their eyes connected. Her stride faltered.

'I'll wait for you,' he said, mentally rescheduling all the things he was meant to do today. The pursuit of ownership of Rozendal was more important. 'Then I'll drive you over to Rozendal.'

Her reply was a toss of her head which dislodged some of the heavy mass of her hair so that it tumbled down her back, a vivid autumnal cascade against the snowy white fabric of the bathrobe. He didn't know if that was an acceptance or a rejection of his offer, but he was prepared to wait for as long as it took to find out.

Scarlett let the robe slip from her shoulders, shed her underwear and turned the shower onto the highest setting. The spray stung like needles on her skin. She tipped her head back, letting the water stream over her face before tugging the scrunchie from her hair.

Will might be waiting for her but she was not going to hurry. She was unlikely to be able to have another shower like this for a while. She'd seen the plumbing arrangements at Rozendal and her expectations were zero.

Bathing in an iron tub in front of a fire might become the height of luxury, at least for a few weeks.

That would not stop her. On numerous expeditions to some of the most remote places on earth she'd showered under buckets suspended from trees, leapt from scalding saunas into icy lakes, or rolled in snow, or swum beneath waterfalls. None of those options had featured four walls or a roof.

Finally, clean and polished from head to toe, courtesy of the array of expensive products lined up on a shelf in the shower, she stepped onto the marble floor of the bathroom and enveloped herself in one of the oversized thick towels which hung from a heated rail.

Studying the contents of her small suitcase, she wondered where her head had been when her hands were packing it. She couldn't remember. She pulled out a fresh pair of jeans and a cotton shirt, applied some sunscreen and lip balm and wove her damp hair into a chunky French plait. Concealer was not much use against the purple smudges of fatigue which lingered beneath her eyes, but tucked into the battered canvas espadrilles at the bottom of the case she found her perfume. Spritzing some onto her wrists and neck instantly made her feel better.

Yes, she was tired, and she had to keep her eyes averted from the bed in case its allure became too great to resist, but she felt purpose and determination rising through her again. Will hadn't mentioned his disappointment at failing to buy Rozendal, but she was sure he hadn't given up his plan. When he made a move, she'd be ready for him.

It seemed Will hadn't waited. He'd gone away and come back again. At the foot of the steps, behind her small hire car, stood a dark green Range Rover, and leaning against the passenger side door, his arms folded across that broad chest and his eyes hidden behind shades, was Will, looking as if he was prepared to wait all day.

He straightened up as she ran down the steps, turning to open the door for her. As he slid into the driver's seat, he glanced across at her.

'Better?'

Scarlett nodded. She knew she looked better,

but his acknowledgment of it brought a flush of warmth to her cheeks.

She noticed how his hands looked light but sure on the wheel and she thought, suddenly, that they would bring the same gentle, confident touch to anything else—an animal…a piece of beloved old furniture…a woman's body.

Not like Alan at all. His touch had been far from gentle. Never unrushed. He had made her feel tense and anxious and then suggested that she was cold and unresponsive.

She shook her head to break her train of thought. She was determined not to need to feel a man's touch again, because she never planned to be in a relationship again. Relationships were the quickest route to heartbreak and disappointment, and she'd had her fill of those. Plants and animals were much more reliable and rewarding than humans. They generally behaved as you expected them to and repaid any care and attention you gave them with devotion and beauty.

Will swung the big vehicle into a bend and Scarlett reached up and held the handle above the door. As they crested a hill, clouds of dust billowing behind them, she saw Rozendal from above for the first time.

It looked more magical than she remembered: a Sleeping Beauty of a house and grounds, waiting for her to bring them back to lush and productive life. Excitement and anticipation unfurled in her stomach and she leaned forward in her seat, watching the property grow nearer as they descended the hill.

Will didn't pull up at the back steps as she'd expected him to. He continued around the side of the Manor and finally stopped on the barely visible gravel turning circle at the foot of the sweeping front steps. Scarlett had a vague recollection of scrambling up those very steps the day before, racing against time. In her haste, she hadn't taken a single second to study the building and later it had been the view that mesmerised her. And by the time she'd walked through the shuttered rooms, amongst the shrouded furniture, she'd been too tired to notice much.

She pushed open the car door and slid out, her feet hitting the tangle of weeds which pushed up through the gravel. Her eyes travelled up the crumbling steps to the wraparound veranda propped up on leaning posts, over the walls covered in cracked plaster and the shutters hanging at drunken angles off their hinges. She saw the moss growing on the thatch and the tree growing out through a hole in it. Perhaps disturbed by their arrival, a flock of pigeons erupted from a different part of the roof, but the large crow, perched on one of the crooked chimneys, one beady eye bent on her, remained at its post, cawing its disapproval.

Scarlett put a hand to her mouth. 'Oh…'

CHAPTER SEVEN

SCARLETT GLANCED OVER her shoulder at Will, who was walking around the front of the car, towards her. She dropped her hand.

'Oh!' she exclaimed again, this time trying to sound delighted rather than deeply dismayed. 'It's so…so…it's so *beautiful*.'

If he thought she was shocked or having second thoughts about her plans for the estate, he would most likely try to take advantage of her—push forward his own ideas and reasons for wanting to buy Rozendal. He was bossy—he'd admitted to that—and he could probably be very, very persuasive. He'd already shown he could get her to do the things he asked, even though most of them had been for her own good. Sleep at Bellevale, take sugar in her coffee, accept his offer of a ride to Rozendal. She'd resisted all those suggestions, but she'd given in. She wouldn't be doing that again.

He was obviously a man who expected to get what he wanted. She wondered if anyone had ever said no to him and stuck to it. If not, she planned to be the first.

So she conjured up her most enthusiastic expression and switched on her widest smile.

'Isn't it just the most perfect house you've ever

seen?' She began to pick her way towards the foot of the steps.

'I'm afraid I can't agree with you, Scarlett. Architecturally, I think Bellevale is the better house, and it's structurally sound...'

'You're entitled to your opinion, naturally. And of course Bellevale is structurally sound. It hasn't been neglected like this.' She swept her arm in a wide arc, encompassing the house and surrounding wilderness that had once been a garden. 'But when Rozendal has been renovated and the grounds restored, it will be unbeatable.'

She hoped she sounded convincing, because the closer she got to the top of the steps, the more devastation she saw and the lower her heart sank. This wasn't something that a lick of paint and a carpenter with a hammer and nails could mend. It was going to take a team of specialists and many months to make it habitable.

The romantic vision of bathing in a hipbath before a roaring fire fizzled and died. If she could get that rusty tap above the stone water trough at the side of the house fixed, perhaps she could wash there.

Will had followed her up the steps and stood behind her, no doubt waiting for her to throw up her hands in defeat. Then he would dive in with an offer to take the place off her, free her of the liability.

There was no way in the world she would be walking away from this. Marguerite had wanted her to have it and it was her home. Her *only* home.

That feeling of belonging flooded back through her body, filling her heart to overflowing. It was as if she was already putting down roots, like the trees and plants she intended to introduce to the gardens would do.

She turned to look at Will. He'd removed his sunglasses and his gaze was searching as her eyes met his.

'Scarlett…'

'What?' She twisted round and pushed against the door. It creaked open, just as it had done yesterday, when it had revealed the hall full of people, the auctioneer with his raised gavel.

'You don't have to do this.' He shook his head, his eyes dark. 'It's an impossible task.'

She walked into the house. Shafts of sunlight angled through the tall windows, their multi-paned squares creating geometric patterns on the dusty floor. She could see her footprints on the stairs. The set going up were of her trainers. The one coming down was of her bare feet. Those prints felt like the stamp of ownership. *Her* ownership.

This house had been given to her to care for and she would not neglect her duty. She knew how that felt. How promises could be broken. How love which you took for granted could prove as fickle as a butterfly, flitting from one flower to the next and never fully committing to any of them.

She would never be guilty of that. She loved

this house, the garden, the whole valley, and her love would be for ever.

'And yet…' she said to Will, who stood in the doorway, his wide shoulders blocking the light, a ray of sun glinting off his dark hair, his expression grim. 'And yet you were prepared to do it. Just yesterday. If I hadn't turned up and stopped the auction at nine seconds before midday, you'd now be the owner of Rozendal. If it's such a disaster, why did you want it so badly, if at all?'

Without waiting for an answer, she threaded her way through the collection of chairs which had been randomly placed for the punters who'd attended the auction and hooked Will's jacket off the back of one of them, holding it out to him.

'Your jacket. You left it here yesterday.'

Will took it and immediately put it down on a different chair. 'Shall we go through to the kitchen? I think it's slightly more civilised in there.'

'I'll follow you. You said you could show me which floorboards are safe to walk on.'

He didn't reply but led the way through the dark house and in the kitchen pulled out two chairs at the weathered oak table. They sat facing one another.

'Please explain to me why you want to do this, Scarlett, so that I can talk you out of it.'

Scarlett pulled her feet up onto the chair and hugged her knees. She bit her lip. How much should she explain? He'd saved her from tumbling

into the cellar last night and given her a comfortable bed and a life-saving breakfast.

Did that mean she had to tell him everything? No,
she didn't think so. Not everything. But she could
tell him enough to try to make him understand.

'I feel as if this is my home,' she said. 'As if I
belong here.'

Will folded his arms and rested them on the
table. She felt the force of his intense focus as
his eyes drilled into hers, demanding an answer.

'But you must have a home in London. Or at
least in England.'

'What makes you say that?'

'You've obviously grown up there. It's logical
to assume you'd have a home. A job. Family?'

A couple of weeks ago Scarlett would have said
she had most of those things. The speed with which
it had all crumbled still shocked her. But Will didn't
need to know about that.

'I've never been part of a proper family. My
parents,' she said, 'didn't intend to have children.
They were as careless about that as they turned
out to be about most things, and I was a surprise.
Not a pleasant one. Their plans for seeing the
world together had to be put on hold and they did
not include a plus one. They muddled through
childcare for a few years but when I was eight and
they felt they'd done their bit in raising me, they
sent me to boarding school.'

Will shifted on his chair and ran a hand over

his jaw. 'I also went to boarding school,' he said. 'I loved it.'

Scarlett nodded. 'Okay. But I didn't. I was used to solitude. I missed having my own room, with my books and toys, where I spent a lot of time, but my Mum and Dad said school wouldn't be for long. They wanted to travel, but they'd be back to take me home for the holidays.' She picked at a knot in the denim stretched over her knees. 'Only they didn't come back. They sent a message to say they were stuck in Kathmandu, held up by floods, and I had to stay at school, with a couple of resentful teachers looking after me.'

'That's unfortunate. But it was just for one holiday, right?'

'Actually, no. I think they realised how easy it was, just to leave me there. Luckily, it wasn't possible to stay at school through the summer holidays, so my guardian and godmother, Marguerite du Valois, was contacted and asked to take me away. I hardly knew her. She was the original eccentric older spinster godmother. She was shocked to discover what had happened, and she set about changing things.' Scarlett nibbled at her bottom lip. 'Days spent with Marguerite were unpredictable but never, ever boring.'

'Good. But I don't see how that is relevant to you wanting to take on the restoration of this falling-down house.'

'I discovered my parents had sold their house to

fund their travels and my school fees. The bedroom I imagined returning to was no longer mine. My toys had been given to charity, along with my books.'

Scarlett felt the pain and anger of that revelation as if it had happened yesterday. She'd kept it a secret from the friends she'd made at school. The romantic narrative she'd woven around her parents' absence had become shallow and false. How could she say they were on an important scientific research expedition in the Himalayas, tracking snow leopards, when she suspected they were sipping cocktails on a beach in Thailand?

'But you must still see them? Unless they're…'

'Oh, they're still alive, and no, I don't see them. They showed no interest in me from the day they drove away through the school gates. They never wanted children, and they'd found the perfect solution for dealing with the child they'd had by accident.'

'They never once came back to see you? That's hard to believe.'

Scarlett felt heat explode in her cheeks, but it was the heat of shame, not embarrassment. All these years later, and the memory could still do this to her.

'My father came back. But I was thirteen by then, and I told him never to come again.'

Will's blue eyes widened and his eyebrows rose. 'Why?'

She puffed out a breath and linked her fingers

around her knees again, gazing past him, out to the overgrown garden and the mountains beyond. Just looking at their solid, massive shapes gave her a sense of permanence she'd never experienced before.

'He decided school sports day was a good time to show up with his new girlfriend. She looked closer in age to me than to him. It turned out that instead of finding each other on their travels, my parents had each found someone else. He tried to show his new love interest how young and athletic he was by running in the fathers' race, but he twisted his ankle.' She exhaled slowly, trying to tame her heartbeat. 'I wanted to dig a hole for myself and hide away in it for ever. That's when I told him never to come back.'

'And he never did?'

'No, but his parting shot as he was carted off in an ambulance was that my mother had a new partner too. She'd moved in with her guru in India and was learning to meditate and play the sitar.'

Will's chair scraped across the tiled floor as he pushed it back. Scarlett watched him pace across to one of the windows. He stood with his back to her, his hands in his pockets. It should have been a relaxed stance, but she could see the tense muscles of his shoulders under the taut fabric of his shirt. He turned, dipped his head and ran a hand across the back of his neck.

She had a vivid flashback of him making the

same gesture almost exactly twenty-four hours ago, as the ownership of Rozendal slipped from his grasp. Was it an expression of frustration? Anger?

'I'm sorry,' he said.

'Neither of their new relationships lasted and they eventually got back together again.' Scarlett lifted her shoulders.

'You're in touch with them?' He sounded surprised.

She hesitated. 'No...but they can find me through Marguerite's solicitor.'

'That is a very sad story.'

'Don't be sad on my behalf. I was lucky to have Marguerite. She was a great mentor and she helped me to make good choices.' She dropped her eyes, unable to hold his gaze any longer. 'Mostly.'

The pause before he spoke again was slightly too long.

'Did you have any idea about this house? That she was leaving it to you?'

'None at all.' She shook her head and pushed her plait over one shoulder. 'She'd told me stories about the house. They always began with: "There is an old house called Rozendal in a hidden valley at the furthest tip of Africa..." but I always thought it something very much from the past. I didn't know she owned it.'

She glanced around the kitchen, taking a moment to see it properly for the first time. It could be a wonderful room, she thought: the hub of the home.

There was a large antiquated range in the fireplace, rows of cupboards along the walls and the huge sink where she'd tested the water supply last night. She could imagine how the ochre floor tiles would gleam once they'd been cleaned and polished, and how the copper pans and brass taps would shine.

Will's gaze followed hers. 'She can't have known it had fallen into such a state of disrepair. Otherwise, surely she'd have left you her house in England instead...'

'That had to be sold to fund her care. Over the past few years I think she'd forgotten all about Rozendal. She had dementia.'

'I see. I'm sorry.' He nodded. 'So you weren't expecting this legacy. I can't believe she would have knowingly burdened you with it.' He crossed back to the table and stood looking down at her.

'It's not a burden, but it was a surprise. A shock. Especially coming so soon after...' She looked away, not wanting him to read her expression, but she wasn't quick enough.

'So soon after what? What happened? Was it something in the Amazon?'

He was worryingly astute, and she bent her head, dismayed by the emotion she felt welling up inside her like a dark tide of hurt and despair, and something else she'd tried so hard to push away: loneliness. She'd lost two people she'd loved and the thought of loving anyone again felt terrifying, and that made her feel not just lonely but *alone*. How comforting it would be to know that someone had her back, to be able to lean into someone for a hug, to feel the warmth of someone's care, just for a moment.

She had to control these feelings because giving in to them was much too dangerous. If Will detected weakness in her he'd think he could persuade her to sell, and she didn't feel strong enough yet to argue with him.

'It's nothing,' she said, aware that her voice was muffled, and knowing he would read all sorts of things into that. 'Nothing that concerns you, anyway.'

'Hey.' His voice had dropped and the word was soft. 'As I see it, you're very much my concern. I am your only neighbour, and you can't do this on your own, if at all.'

Scarlett felt the light touch of his hand on her shoulder. She flinched and pushed her feet to the floor, refusing to admit that his concern was exactly what she craved. Standing up, keeping her back to him, she scrabbled in her pocket for the scrunched-up tissue she was sure she'd find there.

With gentle pressure, Will turned her to face him. There was no hiding the tears that brimmed in her eyes now, or her tremulous bottom lip. The pad of his thumb brushed her cheek.

In the dim kitchen, his eyes were navy blue, the planes of his face shadowed. There was a small scar on his right cheekbone.

'Scarlett,' he said. 'Let me help you.'

CHAPTER EIGHT

WILL WISHED HE could retract those words, or at least reframe them. What if Scarlett thought he meant he could help her to renovate Rozendal? What if she said yes, and asked him for funding to get the project started?

What he wanted her to understand was that he could help her get rid of it.

But he couldn't find the words to express his intention. He was too close to her. Touching her, even just her cheek, had been a big mistake. Her skin was as soft as he'd imagined it would be, and he'd been imagining it way too much since yesterday. It was like stroking a rose petal, not that he'd ever actually done that.

Her eyes glistened and she blinked, but the tears collected, sparkling like tiny diamonds on her lashes.

Her thin shoulder shook and he slipped his hand across her back, splaying it against her shoulder blades, his eyes fixed on her full lower lip.

'Will...'

'Mmm? It's okay.'

Desire rolled over him, hot and urgent, sweeping aside his better judgement, drowning the voice of reason in his head which told him this was a bad—a *very* bad—idea. He *needed* to feel her body against his, to taste her mouth and to inhale that intoxicating scent so deeply he'd never forget it.

It was cool in the old kitchen, on the shady south side of the house, which made the heat spiralling through him even more shocking. Outside, the midday sun blazed from the high African sky, shimmering off the leaves of the trees and bouncing off the mountain crags. The grape harvest was over. The last of the harvest festivities had finished at least a month ago. It was a quiet time in the vineyards, but the rest of the estate was still busy.

He should have been out there, keeping his fingers on all the buttons, all the balls in the air, but none of it mattered. Time had compressed and his awareness shrunk to this place, this moment, and he wanted to freeze it right here. He didn't want it to end.

He stepped closer to Scarlett, pressing his hand against her back, and slid his thumb over her mouth and down to the place above her collarbone where he felt her pulse jumping under his touch.

Her shoulder blades tensed under his hand as she raised her head and placed her hand flat against his chest, but instead of pushing him away she slipped the hand upwards, over his shoulder, to the back of his neck and twisted her fingers into his hair.

For a few seconds his mouth hovered a fraction above hers as he tried to make sense of the longing he saw in the deep pools of her eyes. Then he lowered his head.

She tasted of coffee and almonds and powdered sugar. He tried to hold back, to be gentle and tentative, but he slanted his mouth across hers, knowing the battle was all but lost already. Cupping her head in the palm of his hand, he felt her lips part beneath his and the kiss deepened as she responded to him. Need, all-consuming, throbbed through him, leaving his brain wiped clean of anything but the feel of her body in his arms and the taste of her in his mouth.

Her fingers in his hair tugged him down harder and the small sound of her own need he heard in her throat took him even closer to his limit. He felt the edge of the table behind him and leaned into it, pulling her between his thighs, clamping a hand in the small of her back to hold her steady.

Still he kissed her, exploring the warm sweetness of her mouth, feeling his limbs weakening with desire, his lungs beginning to burn, but refusing to raise his head and break this incredible connection. It was everything he never allowed himself to have, everything he wouldn't let himself feel, and he wanted it to go on for ever. This was all he wanted—all he'd ever need.

But suddenly her hands were on his shoulders, and this time she was pushing him away. For a few dazed seconds he tried to resist, tightening his arms around her, keeping their lips sealed together, but then she tore her mouth from under his and he let her go.

She stepped back, hands on her cheeks, shaking her head.

'No. No, Will.'

He sucked in a long, shaky breath, bewildered, trying to reconnect with his surroundings, which felt dangerously unstable. He'd been transported to somewhere he didn't recognise but where he'd felt infinitely safe, and he didn't want to come back to this world which was tipping on its axis. He'd never experienced the feeling that nothing—*nothing*—outside the moment mattered. Control of his life, of his surroundings, above all, of his emotions, was what he valued above all else. The thought that he could lose it in a few seconds in the arms of a woman he barely knew was unbelievable.

It was deeply disturbing.

'Scarlett, I'm…sorry. That shouldn't…'

Then he realised she was looking beyond him, towards the door to the back steps. He'd kicked it closed last night, he remembered, as he'd cradled Scarlett, asleep in his arms, and carried her to his car. He spun round. The door was open.

'Is anyone here?' Grace's melodious voice called as she appeared, an elegant silhouette against the backdrop of bright sunshine. She stopped on the threshold, her hand raised, about to tug on the frayed length of old rope which hung beneath the brass bell beside the wooden door. 'Will?'

He heard Scarlett's soft gasp and then she stepped round him and ran towards the door like a trapped bird escaping from a dark cage and fleeing towards the light. She bumped into Grace and then disappeared, down the steps.

'Grace?' Will swiped a hand over his jaw. 'What are you doing here?' Stupid question, he realised, and she could ask the same of him. She was probably kindly checking up on Scarlett, whereas *he*… what the hell *was* he doing here?

This sensation of confusion was totally alien to him. He shook his head, trying to find his mental balance. Finding his physical balance was going to be a lot more difficult. He tried to drag his mind back to the present, away from his clamouring body, but he found he was looking to where Scarlett had vanished, wanting to go after her, to finish what they'd started…

Grace walked into the room and stopped, folding her arms.

'What was *that* all about?'

Will pulled shaking fingers over his face, wondering how much his unguarded expression had given away.

'I… I…offered…*suggested*…that she might let me help her with this…situation.' He shoved his hands into his pockets.

'And what was her response to that?'

'She…got a little…emotional.'

'A *little* emotional? Then how come you look like you've been on the receiving end of bad news and she looked like she'd been kissed? Very thoroughly kissed.'

'I was trying to comfort her. It got out of hand. Hell, Grace, that shouldn't have happened. Especially not with her.'

Grace turned and rested her hips against the table. 'What do you mean?'

'She's…vulnerable. A lot has happened in her life. Most of it not good. And that's not counting something I think happened in the Amazon, which she's not talking about.'

'The *Amazon*? Will, are you sure you're okay? You're not making much sense.'

'It's a long story, and she hasn't even told me the Amazon part of it. I just know…'

'Will,' Grace said slowly, 'can you look me in the eye and tell me your aim is to pursue the ownership of this estate? Not the *owner*? Because from the look on your face, and from what I think I interrupted…'

He stared at her, allowing her words to sink in. He could understand why she'd asked the question. The scene she'd come upon must have looked compromising, even if she hadn't witnessed that kiss. Just thinking about it tightened the muscles of his stomach and made him want to do it again.

'For God's sake, get a grip,' he muttered under his breath.

'What?'

His jaw clenched. 'Nothing. But I need to find her. I must apologise.'

'Apologise for what, Will? Didn't she kiss you back? Did she have to fight you off?'

He thought about how she'd pulled his head down towards her, and the urgency of her mouth under his, her soft sound of desire and the look of bewildered longing in her eyes, and shook his head.

'She kissed me back, but then she…as soon as she wanted to stop, I let her go. But I need to apologise for taking advantage of her. She's tired, in a foreign country, surrounded by strangers. I need to find her *now.'*

Scarlett ran headlong down the uneven steps, praying she would not trip and fall but not slowing her pace. She leapt down the last three and kept on running.

The range of dilapidated buildings behind the house looked like a coach house and stables so she supposed this was the stable yard. *Her* stable yard. The buildings were in an even worse state than the house, but she refused to confront that fact now. This was already all too overwhelming.

And what had just happened with Will had pushed her fragile emotions from teetering on the edge of uncontrollable over into the dark regions of completely unmanageable. She could not deal with those feelings, alongside everything else, right now.

Why, *why*, had she let that happen? She'd promised herself—sworn—that no man would take advantage of her ever again. She'd met Alan when she'd been vulnerable and lost. Marguerite had been vanishing before her eyes, into the frightening, fractured world of dementia. The house had been sold to provide for her care and she, Scarlett, had taken a research job based in London so she could visit her. She'd moved into a basement room in a flat-share in Hackney.

Alan had been one of the leading botanists at the facility, responsible for organising expeditions to remote and lost places, mapping the positions of rare and endangered plants, and he'd quickly taken her under his determined wing.

Some of her colleagues had joked that her brain was the attraction, which, they'd suggested, was superior to Alan's own, but she hadn't believed them. At a time when she'd lost her home and the person who'd been mother, friend and partner in hair-raising escapades all over the country to her, she'd felt warmed and validated by his attention.

He'd made her feel needed and safe. He'd offered security when, for the second time in her life, she'd lost hers. When he'd suggested she move into his South Kensington flat with him, she'd been flattered. Looking back, with the acuity of hindsight, she wondered how she'd so easily let go of the independence Marguerite had fostered in her. Alan had presented solutions to her problems and she'd accepted all of them without question. It had felt so simple. Only after it all fell apart had she realised she'd exchanged her free spirit for a level of control she'd found suffocating.

Love, she'd decided, was never straightforward or unconditional. Accepting or giving it came with the possibility of rejection and the need to compromise. She'd learned at the age of eight that trust meant different things to different people. How could she have forgotten?

The news that she'd inherited Rozendal had come when she was at her lowest ebb. It had galvanised her into frantic action, filled her with a renewed purpose. From now on she'd be independent, relying only on herself. She'd make bold, brave decisions and stick to them. She would not be swayed or undermined.

Instead of that, she felt overwhelmed by the scale of the task Marguerite had bequeathed her and she'd allowed a man, who she knew for a fact wanted to wrest the ownership of Rozendal from her, to reduce her to a trembling mess of desire and need and longing with one single kiss: a kiss which she'd wanted desperately, because she'd believed it would make her forget, for a few brief moments.

She was angry with herself, and very ashamed.

And she was furious with Will for being able to crush her defences so easily. If nothing else, that fury would help her to rebuild them, twice as strong, and keep her firmly on the path she'd chosen.

Rubbing a hand across her eyes to scrub away the tears which threatened to blind her, she kept running. This was a monumental undertaking, but she would not give up on it, or give it away to someone else. The vision which had sprung into her imagination, fully formed, of a restored house and rewilded estate, was hers alone. No one else, least of all Will, with his no doubt scientific farming methods, immaculate rows of vines and fancy restaurant and holiday cottages, would be able to bring it to fruition. She *must* do it herself. It would give her purpose, restore the self-belief she'd lost.

Beneath the determination to see her dream become reality lurked another reason. She had to keep up the momentum which had sent her racing to catch that flight to Cape Town to claim Rozendal. If she stopped to consider her position for a moment she might waver, and that would plunge her back into the state of fear which had swamped her when she'd been lost in the jungle. She couldn't afford the time or energy to dwell on that.

Sheer willpower and refusal to give in to panic had got her through that ordeal. It would get her through this too, if she kept that corrosive fear locked out.

Finally, her lungs burning, she stumbled to a stop, bent forwards with her hands braced on her knees and tried to catch her breath.

The valley drowsed in the afternoon warmth, unfamiliar birdsong and a faint rustling in the undergrowth the only sounds.

When she straightened up she realised her flight had taken her into the old rose garden. The formal gravel paths were almost invisible under the rampant weeds, but the shape of some of the beds was almost discernible. Roses which hadn't been pruned for decades sent long stems arching against the sky, above the tangled undergrowth. Fighting her way through the thorny branches, she eventually came to a stone fountain at the centre of the symmetrical space. The octagonal basin was dry and choked with dead leaves, but a bronze cherub which stood on a plinth at the centre, holding a conch shell from which water had once poured, was intact.

This, thought Scarlett fiercely, was where she would begin. And she'd begin now.

She pushed up the sleeves of her shirt and began to scoop out armfuls of dead vegetation, the accumulation of years of neglect, dumping it on the path beside her. She needed a wheelbarrow, she thought feverishly, so that she could cart it all away and put it... She'd have to establish a compost heap. Eventually, the goodness from all these leaves would be put back into the soil in the form of organic mulch. The garden would bloom again. Wildlife would flourish.

That was where Will found her.

'Scarlett.'

She'd been so engrossed in tackling her task head-on that she hadn't heard him approach. She hesitated for a second before continuing to scoop out the crisp dead leaves, ignoring him.

'Scarlett?' He was closer. From the corner of her eye she could see the hems of his narrow jeans, his leather boots, scuffed with wear. She considered offloading an armful of leaves onto them. She wished he'd go away and leave her alone.

'You don't have to look at me, Scarlett, if you don't want to. But I'm not going anywhere until you've listened to what I want to say.'

She shook her head and her plait dropped over her shoulder. 'I don't want to hear anything you want to say,' she said through gritted teeth. 'Please go away.'

His feet moved out of sight, and she released a breath of relief.

'No,' he said, his voice quiet. 'I'm not going away.'

She realised he'd sat down on the edge of the stone basin. She straightened up and dusted her hands together, then looked at him.

Immediately, she wished she hadn't. His gaze

was steady. It made her think of the ocean on a calm summer's day, and she wanted her thoughts to be stormy and dark, to fuel the anger she felt towards him.

'I don't think you have anything to say to me, Will. Or me to you. What happened—' she glanced in what she thought was the direction of the house '—back there was a mistake which I won't repeat. If you thought you might somehow persuade me to change my mind by...'

'No,' he interrupted. 'That wasn't... I don't know how it happened, but I'm sorry.'

Scarlett had not expected an apology. If anything, she'd thought he might have followed her to continue his campaign to convince her she couldn't do this. To help her by offering to buy her out. She wiped her hands down the backs of her thighs and raised her eyes to take in the ageless beauty of the valley and the mountains. She belonged here. The thought steadied her.

'You must have noticed,' she said, risking another glance at his face, 'that it wasn't one-sided.' His mouth was set in a firm, straight line and a frown creased the space between those arresting eyes. She wondered how that mouth, so sombre now, could have elicited that explosion of pleasure and desire in her body. How could a simple kiss do that?

She dragged her eyes from his face but they landed on his hands, loosely clasped together between his knees. Those hands had worked their own magic. She still felt the imprint of his fingers in her lower back, and on the place near her collarbone where her wild pulse had betrayed her.

He nodded. 'Yes. I noticed. But that doesn't excuse what I did and I'm sorry.'

'Are you? Or were your actions deliberate? I was already upset, so did you think you might erode my defences even further and begin to persuade me that I can't do this?' She gestured towards the fountain. 'Because if you did, you're wrong. I've already begun.'

She bent to resume clearing the leaves.

'Scarlett, please listen to me. Just for a moment.'

She stood again and shoved her hands into her pockets, biting her bottom lip. 'Will you promise to leave me alone when you've finished?' His hesitation was slight, but she saw it. *'Promise?'*

'Okay. If you want me to.'

'I'm listening.'

He sucked in a deep breath, leaning back, bracing his arms. His shoulders widened and he looked up at her, the sun glinting on his rumpled hair.

'At that moment, Scarlett, there was nothing on my mind beyond the hope that you would not stop kissing me. You were upset. I offered to help you, and I'm prepared to repeat that offer. All I can say in my defence is that I wanted to comfort you. After that, things became a bit hazy.'

'If Grace hadn't come…' She remembered the grip of his thighs on hers as he'd pulled her close, the heat of his body. 'What did you tell her? Or didn't she ask?' She kicked at a clump of daisies with the toe of her shoe.

'She asked. I told her what I've told you. I wanted to comfort you and I don't regret that, although I'm sorry it got out of hand.'

She nodded. Was that what he thought had happened? It'd got out of hand. Such an ordinary phrase to describe the emotions and sensations which had taken hold of her. The feel of the slide of his tongue against hers, the liquefying of her limbs until she thought she'd fall if he released her, the overpowering single thought that had occupied her brain: she needed more of him.

'How,' she asked, 'were you offering to help?' She wondered if he thought she'd ask him for money. 'Because I'm intrigued to know.'

Will stood up and took a few paces away from her. He bent to pick up a handful of the dead leaves she'd removed from the fountain and crushed them in his fist, letting the shredded flakes sift through his fingers to the ground.

'Look around you, Scarlett. Not just at the rose garden, but at the rest of the estate. At the barns and stables, and the cart lodge.'

Cart lodge, she thought. *Not coach house.*

'And look at the house. I mean *really* look at it. See it for what it is, not for what you wish it was.

Restoring all this is an insurmountable task for one woman on her own. It'd take teams of builders and landscape designers, contractors, gardeners and labourers to wrest this place back from nature and make it habitable again. I can make you an offer for twice what I was going to pay for it at the auction yesterday. You can return to your life and work in London, buy yourself a house, live a comfortable life instead of...' He looked around. 'Instead of taking on this impossible project. Please consider it.'

Scarlett studied him. His frown had deepened, and he looked a little pale under his tan. He sounded utterly sincere. Was this really because he feared for her well-being and sanity, or was there some other, more fundamental reason why he wanted Rozendal so badly? Was it just that he'd decided it should be his, and he wouldn't give up until he had what he wanted? According to Marguerite, the other estate in the valley had been in the hands of the same family for longer than Rozendal had belonged to hers.

Will had lived with the certainty of his place in the world all his life. He was rooted in this soil as deeply as the ancient oaks and gnarled vines in the vineyards. He'd never had to wonder where he belonged. He'd always known.

The anger she was nurturing expanded in her chest. She breathed in and out several times, counting backwards in her head.

'If you'll just think…' he said again. 'Try to understand…'

Scarlett gave up the fight. 'I am thinking,' she said. 'And what I'm thinking…' Her voice rose. 'What I'm thinking is that it's you, Will Duvinage, who needs to try to understand something. Because you don't understand at all, do you?'

'Understand what?' He looked shocked, either by her raised voice or by her suggestion. She didn't know which and she didn't care.

'Understand what it's like not belonging. Not *belonging* anywhere. You've lived here all your life. *All your life!* Do you know what that sounds like to me? It sounds like paradise. You've never had to question your right to be here. Probably the furthest away you've ever lived was at boarding school. And I'm willing to bet your parents came to every speech day, every sports day, every match, and turned up on the last day of term to bring you home for the holidays. *Home!*'

'Scarlett…'

She shook her head, taking a ragged breath. 'You've never had to doubt whether this is the life you wanted or deserved. It's been your entitlement since you were born, and the entitlement of all your ancestors, going back centuries.'

She was shouting now, her heart racing, her breath coming in gasps. 'And because of that… *entitlement*…because everything has always been exactly as you wanted it, you believe you can force me into selling Rozendal to you, because you want it. How neat it would have been for you to have bought it yesterday, only I came along and spoilt things. You already have so much. Why must you have Rozendal too…?'

'Scarlett, stop. Please.' He held up a hand, but she was on a roll.

'If you think you're going to take this from me, you're wrong. Marguerite wanted me to have Rozendal and I can see why. It's beautiful and special. Magical. And I've decided I want that magic in my life. This is home for me now. The only home that's ever been truly mine, and I'm not giving it up. If I have to live in one room, cook on an open fire, wash outside in a drinking trough, I'm not giving it up.'

She stopped, horrified by the sting of tears gathering in her eyes. She would never give Will the satisfaction of seeing her cry again.

A long charged silence followed her outburst. When he finally spoke she could tell that he was angry too. His voice shook and colour streaked across his sharp cheekbones.

'You don't know what you're talking about, Scarlett. You're wrong.'

'Which bit of what I said was wrong, Will?'

Her voice was a husky whisper. As the adrenalin took hold she began to shake.

He started to speak then shook his head, appearing to change his mind about what he was going to say.

Finally, he drew in a deep breath and exhaled again. Scarlett wondered how she could note the rise and fall of his broad chest and remember how it felt to be held in his arms, against that wall of muscle, when all she wanted was to forget.

'I'm just asking you to think very carefully,' he said, sounding as if he was maintaining a reasonable tone by sheer effort. 'I'm giving you an easy way out of this. If you insist on continuing with your plan, it's going to cost you a fortune.'

Despite the tears that hovered and the sob that threatened to choke her, she smiled. Perhaps he hoped to lend her money and then call in the debt when she could least afford to honour it. He'd have her trapped then, and she'd be forced to sell to him.

Once, she would have taken such an offer at face value. She wouldn't have suspected an ulterior motive. Once, she'd been naïve enough to trust people.

It was sad, acknowledging that her ability to trust had been shaken, rather like admitting there was no such thing as unconditional love. But she'd learnt to be realistic and pragmatic. Not having to accept financial help was a powerful feeling.

'Luckily, I don't need a fortune, Will,' she said softly. 'Because Marguerite left me hers.'

CHAPTER NINE

SCARLETT WATCHED HIM stride away from her, shoving his way through the overgrown garden. She heard him swear. Perhaps he was venting his anger at her. Perhaps he'd been scratched by one of the ancient thorny rose stems. She glanced down at her own scratched forearms.

Drained, she sat on the edge of the fountain, near where Will had been, and rested her elbows on her knees, closing her eyes. Fatigue, her constant shadow for the past ten days, threatened to overwhelm her and for the first time she allowed herself to wonder what she was doing.

But even as doubt stalked her she knew she wouldn't give in. She had to make a success of this. Rozendal was going to become a shining example of the benefits of rewilding, to the landscape, to wildlife and to ecological systems.

She had absolute faith in her dream. She just didn't know how she was going to achieve it. Will was right when he'd said she'd need an army of helpers. How did she go about finding one?

Her tummy rumbled and her mouth was dry. Admitting that she couldn't concentrate while she was hungry and thirsty, she turned her back on the dry fountain, on which she'd hardly made an impression, and began to find her way back to the house.

The Range Rover was gone. That didn't surprise her. She'd have to walk back to Bellevale to collect her car and her luggage and then ask for directions to the nearest food store. Communications with Will would probably be through his lawyer from now on. *One step at a time*, she told herself. *Don't think beyond that.*

She circled the house, stopping to try the corroded tap at the water butt. It was impossibly stiff and made an alarming grating sound. The pipe vibrated violently before a trickle of rusty water splashed into the stone trough.

Back in the kitchen, she folded herself onto one of the wooden chairs and wondered how she could summon up the energy to return on foot to Bellevale. She wasn't at all sure she would be able to find the way. Should she risk a sip of the rusty water at the sink?

But as she pulled herself upright she heard the sound of tyres on gravel. Through the window she saw Will's Range Rover pull up at the foot of the steps. Its own cloud of dust caught up with it, swirling across the stable yard. The rain of the previous night had been torrential, but it had vanished into the parched earth, leaving it as dry as before.

He was the very last person she wanted to see. Wasn't he? Actually, Alan was top of that particular chart, but Will came a close second. Both were entitled men who'd aimed to manipulate her for their own ends.

The uncomfortable heat of an adrenalin rush pumped through her veins as the rhythm of her heartbeat picked up. Fight or flight? She could retreat upstairs, but he'd find her if he came looking. She could…

It was already too late.

Will had pulled a canvas carrier bag from the back and was pounding up the steps as if he was working out on a treadmill.

He stopped in the doorway, his eyes sweeping across the room and landing on her. He nodded, crossed the floor in two long strides and dumped the bag on the table.

'I've brought food. I decided you were hangry.'

'Hangry?'

'Yeah. Hungry and angry. It's a recognised medical condition. Well documented.'

Scarlett eyed the bag. She was hungry. Very hungry. And her anger, which had been off the scale, still simmered beneath her weariness and the doubt which had begun to niggle at her.

'What made you think that?'

Will began to unpack the bag, glancing across at her. 'You're looking at the bag, so I know you're hungry.' She couldn't decide if the spark in his eyes was one of teasing or triumph. 'Besides, you had coffee and pastries hours ago, and you've expended some energy since then.' His eyes flicked from her face to the watch on his wrist and back again. 'Sugar high followed by an energy crash. Dangerous.' He pulled a bottle of water from the bag. 'And it's past lunchtime.' He put a loaf of bread, ham and cheese and a bar of chocolate on the table. Her eyes went to his strong fingers as they flexed and twisted the cap from the water bottle. He offered it to her. 'As for your anger, I've thought about what you said and I can understand why you might have formed your opinions. But that's a discussion I don't intend to have.'

Scarlett accepted the bottle, his fingers brushing against hers, and the memory of his hand cupping the back of her head ambushed her. Those fingertips exerting gentle pressure on her skin had felt…amazing. Exciting. And his mouth… What would it be like to feel those hands, those long, capable fingers and those deft lips, exploring the rest of her body? She closed her eyes. A headache began an insidious throb behind her eyes and she longed for a cup of tea. There was no chance of making one in this kitchen.

Will opened a couple of drawers, humming under his breath, until he found a breadknife, plates and cutlery.

'Give these a wipe, Scarlett.' He dug in the bag for a cloth. 'I think they're only dusty, but it would be sensible to check before using them.' She took the cloth, taking care to avoid his touch this time.

'You're very organised.'

He shook his head as he gripped the loaf and the knife. Scarlett tightened her hold on the plate in her hand, watching the action of the muscles and tendons of his tanned forearms as the blade sliced into the bread.

'I asked Grace to sort out some food from the restaurant kitchen. It's unlikely I would have thought of putting in a cloth.' He peered into the bag. 'Or wine, for that matter.'

He made sandwiches, peeled the wrapper from the chocolate and snapped it into squares. Then he pushed a plate across the table towards her. 'Sit and eat.' He pulled out a chair. 'You'll feel better. Then we can talk.'

'Thank you. You must think I'm hopeless. But normally I'm very good at taking care of myself.'

'It seems you've had a stressful, possibly traumatic time lately.' She saw the searching look in his narrow gaze and dropped her head to bite into a sandwich. 'This—' he gestured around the room '—is a huge change for you. It's not surprising if you're feeling disorientated.'

Scarlett decided to swerve that conversation. 'Is this bread local? It's delicious.'

'It would have been baked in the restaurant kitchen this morning. Grace tells me she's perfected the art of the sourdough loaf.'

'I think I agree.'

'I'll tell her. The food we serve is all local.

There're very few food miles on this table. It's a source of pride at Bellevale, although it can be a challenge too.'

Scarlett felt a stirring of surprise and she tried to adjust her perception of Will. She'd imagined Bellevale to be a state-of-the-art estate, and if asparagus needed to be flown in from Mexico or cheese from France she wouldn't expect him to bother about the air miles.

'I'm surprised you care about things like that.' She swallowed a few mouthfuls of water from her bottle.

'I care about Bellevale. That is my bottom line. And I know that what is good for the planet is going to be good for the estate. That's a no-brainer. The methods we use for farming and winemaking are cutting-edge and world-class. And that goes for every part of the operation. There is always a waiting list for the restaurant and the cottages. The food, service and accommodation are all five-star.' He pushed the chocolate across the table towards Scarlett then leaned back in his chair. 'But we try to ensure, at every stage, that nothing we do is harmful to the environment.'

'And the wine? Obviously, you export. You can't avoid those food miles.'

He nodded. 'You're right. We can't. But our marketing and sales teams spread the message that the estate is ethically run. Visitors, and we have many, are welcome to talk to any member of staff. They will always tell the same story: people love working here because the conditions are excellent. Our organic wines are growing in popularity.'

'It sounds as though you set high standards.' She took a square of chocolate.

'My standards are super-high, but I lead by example and the results speak for themselves.'

'Is that another way of saying you always expect to get your own way?' The chocolate melted on her tongue, smooth and bittersweet with a whisper of flaky salt.

He shook his head. 'I'm reputed to be single-minded and aloof, and I don't dispute that, although I think *determined* is a better word. And if I get my own way, it's because most of the time it's the right way.' His smile was self-deprecating, robbing his words of the arrogance she might have heard in them. 'But,' he continued, 'enough about me. How about you?'

'What about me?'

He chose a chair opposite her, balancing an ankle on a knee and folding his arms across his chest.

'Scarlett.' His tone was softer. 'You're exhausted and stressed. You need to be sensible.'

'I won't change my mind. You'll be wasting your time if you try to make me.'

'I recognise your determination, and I admire that. What *would* be a waste of time would be having to check up on you twice a day to make sure you're okay.'

'Why would you do that?' Surprise made her look up, her eyes locking with his.

'Because we're your only neighbours, and you're on your own. It's how we operate around here. We look out for each other.'

'What do you want me to do? Check into a hotel? Is there one?'

'Yes, there is. It's called Bellevale, although, strictly speaking, it's not a hotel.'

Scarlett shook her head. 'I can't do that.'

'Tell me why not.'

'It would be an imposition. And you and I… we're not on good terms. We'd argue…'

'If it bothers you, you can pay for Vineyard Cottage. It's available for two weeks. And I can help you to get your project up and running.'

'Why would you have any interest in doing that? You don't agree with what I want to do.'

'I'm not sure I fully understand what you intend to do, apart from making this house habitable. If we can sit down and talk about it some time it would be helpful for both of us. Meanwhile, you need to recover. You've suffered a bereavement, had a long flight, a traumatic experience last night. All of that would take its toll on anyone.' His eyes went to her arms, but she'd rolled down the sleeves of her shirt, covering the damaged skin. 'And before that…'

She shook her head, making it clear that subject was not open for discussion.

'Your forehead...'

He rubbed his fingers across his left temple. 'It's just a scratch. Those rose thorns are fierce.'

He was quiet for a minute. Then he stood up and walked over to the ancient fridge in the corner and pulled the door open.

'Mmm. When the power is on this will probably work, after a fashion. The cooker... I'm not sure about that. It looks dangerous. The water is not drinkable and if you wash in it you'll turn a rusty shade of orange all over.'

'Like my hair.'

He turned his head, his eyes resting on her hair. 'Not at all like your hair.' He slammed the fridge shut but it sprang open again. 'Nothing really works. But some of it could be made to work, and I and the team at Bellevale are the people who can make it happen.'

He returned to stand in front of Scarlett, hands in his pockets, rolling his shoulders. 'Give yourself time, Scarlett. There's been a lot going on in your life. You may be strong and independent, but right now you're vulnerable and that's nothing to be defensive about. You're alone, and I feel responsible for you. Your life has changed and that has been a shock, but you showing up unexpectedly like that yesterday was a shock to everyone in the valley too. We all need to adjust. Yes, you have turned my plans upside down, but I'll make new ones.' He paused, shaking his head. 'That's what I've always done.' His voice dropped. 'And some of the changes I've had to make have been huge.'

Scarlett dropped her head into her hands. 'You make it sound as if I have no choice.'

'You do have a choice, but if you choose to stay here it will be difficult for everyone, mostly for you. You'll spend so much time and energy simply surviving that you won't achieve anything else. There's no internet, no phone signal. How are you going to organise anything? Winter is approaching and it'll be cold and wet. Colder and much, much wetter than you probably imagine. We have almost all our annual rainfall in three months and it's not gentle English rain.' He pulled his hands from his pockets and turned his palms upwards. 'Please, Scarlett, be sensible.'

Being sensible, Marguerite had always said, usually meant being boring. She tried to imagine what her godmother would have done in this situation. It wasn't easy. Would she have raised two fingers at Will's offer and toughed it out on her own? If she tried to do that and failed, she'd have to come to Will for help anyway, admitting defeat. The idea rankled.

If she accepted the accommodation at Bellevale, and help from Will now, it wouldn't be for long. If she stayed there just long enough for the roof at Rozendal to be repaired, the power and water supplies to be secured and until she'd been able to hire some help for the garden…

'Scarlett.' His voice sounded strained, as if he was doing his best to hold something back. 'Come home with me. Please.'

Scarlett sighed, pushing her fingertips into her hair and massaging her temples.

'Are you okay?' There was a thread of concern in his voice.

'Yeah. Just…memories.' She didn't have to explain that some of them were old, but some were as recent as this morning. She scraped her chair away from the table and stood up. 'Okay.' She breathed out a long sigh. 'But whatever the state of the house, when I move out of Vineyard Cottage in two weeks I'll move in here. That's not negotiable.'

Relief softened Will's expression. The lines of anxiety faded, and he smiled. 'That's the right decision.'

'And just to be clear, this is not you getting your own way. It's me deciding how to do it.'

His smile vanished, but the amusement in his eyes lingered. 'Of course.'

'You mentioned wine? And the chocolate is *really* good.'

'It's made by a small bean to bar operation in Cape Town. They source their ingredients from sustainable cocoa plantations in West Africa. When they were looking for investors to start up,

I provided a major stake. The company continues to grow.'

Scarlett peered into the bag Will had repacked. 'The wine is in there?'

'It is, but I think it's grown a little warm. Let's head back to Bellevale and pop it into the fridge at Vineyard Cottage. You can have it later.'

'You'll know where I am at Bellevale, so you can avoid me if you want to.'

He hoisted the bag from the table. 'Sure,' he said easily. 'But I won't want to do that.'

'You'll want to know what I'm up to, so you can continue to plot how to get hold of Rozendal.'

'Absolutely.' One corner of his straight mouth lifted, and the trace of a dimple ghosted across his cheek. 'Except I don't plot,' he said, holding her gaze. 'I plan.'

'There's a difference?'

'I think you'll find there is. And I also prefer to meet problems head-on.'

'And I'm a problem for you?'

'More of a challenge.'

CHAPTER TEN

RELIEF MADE WILL breathe more easily as he left the cool kitchen and stepped onto the *stoep* outside the door. He checked to make sure Scarlett was following him. What would he have done if she'd stubbornly refused to take his advice? He knew he could pick her up and carry her, but forcing her would not be acceptable, under any circumstances. But he couldn't have left her here either.

Now he had to let her draw the conclusion that this was the correct decision. He had to try to make things a little easier for her—show his willingness to listen to her plans and to offer any help he could. If he could establish a good working relationship with her, encourage her to trust him, he'd have a much better chance of achieving what he wanted later.

He had already changed his plan.

He had to concentrate on that. His goal was to unite Bellevale and Rozendal. With his sharp business sense and experience, his persuasive tactics, he should be able to do it. She'd agree with him in the end, he was convinced.

What had happened between them this morning had complicated things more than a little.

Her taste, the urgency of her response, had

played havoc with his mind all day and his level of achievement had dropped below what he expected of himself. Way below.

He'd lost count of the number of times his concentration had lapsed, or he'd lost the thread of a conversation, as he tried to identify her scent. Perhaps he could find a way to ask her, without it sounding too personal, although when was asking a woman about her perfume not personal? And why did he think if he knew the answer he'd somehow be able to let go of it?

'There's no key to the door,' he said over his shoulder, 'but close it firmly. You don't want the resident troop of baboons moving in.' He scanned the mountain crags. 'They're probably watching us right now, just waiting for an opportunity.'

'If they're so keen to get in, surely they'd have found a way before now?'

'The house has been abandoned for a long time, but they'll have noticed the human activity here, yesterday and today. Humans mean food to baboons. They'll be down to investigate opportunities for stealing anything they can find.'

He started down the flight of steps, hearing the door close behind him. He slung the bag into the back of the big four-by-four and held the passenger door open for Scarlett.

When she was strapped in and the door was shut he'd relax.

He took the drive slowly, skirting potholes and

bumps on the track and pointing out landmarks on the way.

'When you drive over on your own, look out for that old oak barrel.' He pointed. 'That is where you turn down towards Rozendal. Years ago, it had the name and an arrow painted on the side, but it's illegible now.' He negotiated the turning. 'The sun fades things.'

The road leading to Bellevale was well maintained and Will pressed the accelerator and the vehicle picked up speed. He noticed Scarlett looking around, taking an interest in the landscape, and when he swung the wheel and they turned in between the solid old white gateposts of his home he heard her quiet intake of breath. He glanced across at her.

'Yes, it's beautiful.'

The sight of the avenue of ancient oaks, flanked by acres of immaculate vineyards, never ceased to give him the kick of pleasure he'd been experiencing ever since he could remember. Best of all was the view of the matchless house, the parabolas of its sweeping white gables perfectly symmetrical, the honey-coloured thatch gleaming in the sunshine. It was framed perfectly in the distance. A fountain played in a pool in the middle of the gravel turning circle in front of the homestead, serene white water lilies floating on its surface.

Will took a turning to the left and followed a narrow track between the vineyards, waving to a distant group of workers. They all raised their arms in a salute.

'They're checking the vines for signs of stress or disease.' He hauled the wheel round to the right and pulled up behind Scarlett's hire car, under the giant oak trees. 'We use organic methods of pest control, but we have to be vigilant.' He cut the engine and looked across at Scarlett. 'Vineyard Cottage. Your home for a fortnight.'

Scarlett had slid from her seat before he reached the passenger side of the vehicle. He followed her up the shallow set of steps, reaching around her to open the front door, catching that scent again.

'What...?' he began, but stopped himself. He had to keep this relationship on a business footing. Questions about perfume would never be appropriate. But then his gaze fell on the nape of her neck as she walked through the door ahead of him. The creamy smooth skin was soft, inviting a caress. He knew, because he could still feel the sensation of it at his fingertips. How would it feel, and taste, under his mouth?

Trying to get a grip on the need which stalked through him and making a super-human effort not to haul her into his arms and see what happened next, he carried the grocery bag through to the built-in kitchen in the corner of the open-plan living area.

A packet of tea and a sealed bag of coffee sat next to the kettle. He opened a cupboard to reveal a glass jar of fruited and nutty muesli, alongside pots of local jam and marmalade. The small fridge contained juice, milk, eggs and butter, to which he added the leftovers of Scarlett's late lunch.

In the middle of the small round table an earthenware bowl contained a collection of peaches, plums and apples. Their colours glowed in a shaft of afternoon sunlight. He knew if he opened the brightly coloured tins on the marble worktop he would find them filled with crisp, buttery shortbread and possibly a crumbly fruit cake.

Will straightened up from slotting the bottle of wine into the fridge and closed the door.

'Where did this food come from?'

He lifted his shoulders. 'We always stock the kitchen with basics for our guests.'

'But the guests cancelled. And I'm sure none of this was here this morning. There must have been some mistake.'

Will gave up. 'Okay, I asked Grace to arrange for the cottage to be stocked, as usual. It's no big deal.'

'Maybe not for you. But I can't keep accepting your hospitality. I thought I'd been clear about that.'

'Why? This is just to tide you over. You need to eat, and you probably don't feel like going out, or eating in the restaurant tonight.'

'No, I don't. But every time I accept something from you it puts me in your debt, and that's not a place I want to be.'

'That's not how I see it. This is just our usual way of welcoming guests.'

'Maybe, but I'm not one of your usual guests, am I? And you obviously didn't doubt that I'd agree to come. That is an even bigger problem for me.'

Will strolled over to the window, buying time.

'Why,' he asked eventually, 'is it a problem?' He turned back to face her. She stood in the middle of the room, her hands on her hips, a frown creasing her smooth forehead.

'You seriously can't see why?' She huffed out a breath. 'It's because it means you were confident you'd be able to make me do what you wanted. That you could manipulate me.'

'No.' The shake of his head and his tone were decisive. 'Manipulate is an unpleasant word. It smacks of control and coercion, and that's not how I work. I—*hoped*—I'd be able to persuade you to see that living here for two weeks was the sensible option. And I succeeded.'

He watched, fascinated, as an expression of frustration crossed her features and a spark of emerald flashed in her eyes. Her teeth indented her full lower lip and then the tip of her tongue smoothed over the mark. Her heavy russet plait hung over one shoulder, the blunt end of it, tied in a green ribbon, resting on the curve of her breast.

He found it hard to breathe.

She pushed the braid away, the movement one of contained irritation, and he could see the dip at her throat, where her ivory skin stretched over the tips of her collarbones, moving in and out as she tried to slow her breathing.

If he placed his fingers there, where they'd been earlier today, just above that delicate bone, he knew he'd feel the quick flutter of her pulse. It had been driven by desire, and some other, hidden need. He was sure of that. Now, she was the victim of a different sort of emotion.

She turned on her heel and walked through the door into the bedroom, her plait swinging between her shoulder blades, her hips, curving out from her narrow waist, swaying.

Of course, he knew what she was saying. But if she felt indebted to him, surely that was a good thing? If it made her feel at a disadvantage, so much the better...

His thoughts stalled. He did not want to think about Scarlett at a disadvantage, or in any situation in which she felt indebted or trapped. Her strength and determination were admirable and not something he wanted to be responsible for crushing. He had to be subtle about this. If she no longer wanted to keep Rozendal, Scarlett had to come to the decision on her own. Or she had to believe she had...

He'd help her with her project, but he'd help her see his point of view too.

Her slender figure was silhouetted against the light pouring through the tall window, the slanting rays of the sun illuminating her bright hair. She'd removed her shoes and came, soft-footed, towards him, tugging at the ribbon which fastened the end of her plait. She raised her arms, the cotton fabric of her shirt tugging tight against her breasts, and threaded her fingers through the strands of hair, letting them part and shaking the coppery mass over her shoulders and down her back.

With her full, rosy mouth and the slight flush on the alabaster skin of her cheekbones she looked as if she'd stepped out of a Pre-Raphaelite painting.

Will clenched his fists, his breathing losing its rhythm, wanting it to be *his* fingers easing into her glorious hair.

He had this under control, he told himself. It was a long time since he'd spent more than a few hours with a woman. He always left them safely at their homes or hotels. None of them ever came here, into his personal space.

That didn't mean he couldn't handle this. His self-control was legendary, his determination unshakeable. His mental strength was the reason he was here at all. Contrary to what Scarlett believed, he'd had to fight for Bellevale, the undisputed love of his life, and the fight had been bitter. Taking possession of it had only been the beginning because bringing the estate back to useful productivity had taken several seasons of curtailed sleep and nail-biting uncertainty.

Last year the rains had failed. Farming in Africa,

he reflected, was governed by flood or drought, feast or famine. If the rains this winter weren't sufficient, the harvest would suffer, and so many families depended on their positions here. But now he had a plan.

God, she was beautiful.

He clenched his jaw, gritting his teeth.

If he had this under control, why did he feel he was in so much trouble?

Darkness had fallen, with its African swiftness, beyond Will's study window. He exited the program on his laptop and flipped the lid closed. A strip of light shone beneath the door, and outside a slice of the moon hung above the mountains, tracing their outlines in silver. If he looked the other way, down the valley, he'd see the Southern Cross in the velvety sky.

But his gaze was turned inwards. He tapped his knuckles on the lid of the computer and raked his fingers through his hair, turning over in his mind what he'd read.

What would we do without Google? people often asked. Far more secrets could be kept, he mused. In this case, he wasn't sure that would have been a good thing.

His day had been disrupted and unsatisfactory and he'd come to his study to catch up on some paperwork. But the cause of his disturbed day had continued to get between him and anything else he'd tried to do. His concentration was shot, he'd admitted to himself, unless he was thinking about Scarlett. He had no problem focusing on her at all.

Hell, the thought of her was driving him insane. Kissing her had been one of the sweetest, most erotic experiences of his life, and also one of the most stupid things he'd ever done. The memory of those few intense minutes continued to play havoc with his emotions and his self-control.

As he'd discovered last night, she intrigued him, teased his senses and drove him to unfathomable feelings of protectiveness.

He was a rational, practical man and he didn't understand this irrational and totally unreasonable reaction. He needed to understand her, a little, if he was going to get any peace.

He'd put aside his paperwork, opened his laptop and typed her name into the search engine.

It didn't take long to find her.

She was a botanist. He knew that already. She was highly regarded in her field of research, for her ability to spot minute differences between plants, and had discovered several new species. She'd travelled to some of the most remote, hostile areas of the world. There was a picture of her in the jungle in Borneo, observing wild orangutans.

But the information about her most recent trip to the Amazon was disjointed. The press reports were speculative, in the absence of any verified facts.

Reading between the lines, some of which were

from shouty, sensation-seeking tabloids, she'd been lost in the jungle, feared dead, for six days. A cloud of suspicion hung over the expedition leader, unsubstantiated reports accusing him of abandoning her.

The latest report said she'd returned to England and promptly vanished. She was known to have been staying with a friend in London who now refused to speak to the press, saying only that Scarlett was safe and needed to be left alone.

Will pushed away from his desk and stood up. He needed to think, and he did that best outside. Pulling on a sweater, he left the house, the chill of the autumn evening sharpening his senses and clearing his mind. He took his usual route, around the grounds, to the edge of the vineyards.

The night was still. Bright stars were scattered across the sky and the moon had almost set behind the mountains. High up, among the crags, a jackal barked, the harsh sound echoing through the ravines, and from somewhere close came the double hoot of a Cape Eagle Owl, on the hunt for small mammals.

What was Scarlett running from? Or who had frightened her into disappearing?

Will intended to find out. If he could unravel the mystery surrounding her sudden appearance at Rozendal, he hoped the hold she had taken on his mind and body would loosen.

His walk brought him to the collection of cottages he'd had converted from labourers' quarters to luxury holiday accommodation. He'd built a new, modern complex of houses for his staff, closer to the main road, from where the children could more easily access the bus service to school.

On a normal night he would have turned back towards the Bellevale homestead at that point, but tonight he was drawn onwards, past the cottages, towards the one which stood, secluded and separate from the others.

Vineyard Cottage, so-called because it bordered the vineyards.

The shade of the oaks was deep. He stopped on the edge of it and took a sharp breath.

Scarlett sat on the terrace, under the vine. A candle flickered in a blown-glass shade on the table, throwing dancing shadows across her face. The bottle of wine, frosted with condensation, which he'd put into the fridge earlier, stood open, alongside a half-filled glass. Her hair flowed in a dark, molten mass over her shoulders, and she'd wrapped herself in one of the woollen throws off the sofa, to ward off the cool night air.

He moved forwards, out of the oak shadow, wanting to talk to her but afraid of startling her. Autumn leaves rustled beneath his feet and she turned her head slowly, searching the darkness.

'Scarlett?'

'Will.'

'May I join you?'

CHAPTER ELEVEN

SHE SHOULD HAVE apologised to Will, or at least thanked him.

When she'd watched him walk away from her, vanishing among the thorny bushes, she didn't expect to see him again. But he'd brought lunch to her at Rozendal, and insisted she return to Bellevale with him. Stocking the kitchen had been thoughtful, and she was grateful for the meal she'd put together from the collection of groceries she'd found in the fridge and cupboards.

She'd barely thanked him for either act of kindness. She'd been too busy insisting she could look after herself, that she didn't need his help.

She'd been rude to him and she didn't trust him. He was single-minded, and absolutely focused on what he wanted. All his actions, even if they appeared to be kind and thoughtful, would be geared towards adding Rozendal to the property he already owned.

It would be far too easy to slip into a mindset of believing him, relying on him—*trusting* him.

All these thoughts churned around in her head as she took a long shower, washing away the dust of her battle with the choked fountain. She looked at the wide bed, made up with sumptuous embroidered linen, and knew she was not ready for sleep.

The bottle of wine she'd opened with her meal stood in the fridge, her glass next to the sink, and she gathered them up and opened the door to the terrace.

The night air was cool, almost cold, after the warm day, and she hesitated, but she put the bottle and glass on the table, returned to the living area and pulled the soft woollen throw from the back of the sofa, wrapping herself in its folds. The cream alpaca fabric was as soft and as light as down, enclosing her in a cocoon of warmth and luxurious comfort. She snuggled into the deep cushions of one of the rattan chairs and sipped from her glass.

How unusual to find crystal as fine as this in a holiday cottage. Like everything else, from the throw to the one thousand count linen and the Persian rugs on the oak floors, it lent another layer of opulence to her surroundings.

The wine was exquisite. Crisp and zesty, its fresh notes seemed to help to clear her head. It was one of the Bellevale whites, of course.

The air was still, and the sounds of the African night were unfamiliar to her. Unfamiliar, and completely different from the sounds which had surrounded her in the Amazon.

But the rustle of leaves nearby did not fit. The

disturbance was too loud to be a mouse, or even a snake. The pattern of the noise was unnatural.

It took a second for her to process this. She tensed, annoyed that she'd put herself out here, in a vulnerable position, where she was unlikely to be heard if she called for help.

She eased her head around to face the sound, hoping not to draw attention to herself. The candle on the table gave off very little light so perhaps she'd be invisible to someone prowling in the shadows of the trees.

A shape detached itself from the deep darkness and Will's voice, low and steady, said her name.

She watched him climb the steps. He stopped at the top.

'I'm sorry if I startled you. I was trying not to.'

Scarlett smiled. 'Any dark shape emerging from the trees in the night is going to be at least a little scary, don't you think?' She tipped her head towards the green glass bottle. 'Wine?'

He hesitated for a moment, then nodded. 'Thank you. I'll grab a glass.'

Scarlett pulled the throw more tightly around her shoulders as she waited for him to return.

He poured himself a glass of wine and raised it to her. 'Have you eaten?'

She nodded. 'Yes, thank you, I have.' She took a sip from her glass. 'This wine is excellent. One of yours, obviously.'

Will swallowed a mouthful. 'Mmm. I'm glad

you like it.' He put his glass down and leaned back in his chair, linking his hands behind his head.

'The glasses are pretty special too.'

'Yeah. When we equipped the cottages, I sent buyers round all the antique markets in Cape Town, looking for crystal. Fine wine should be drunk from fine crystal. Sometimes the glasses are mismatched, but personally I think that adds something to the overall feel.'

'The rest of the cottage is beautiful too. Last night…well, last night I hardly woke up enough to know where I was. And this morning I didn't really take much notice. But I've had time now, and every detail is perfect.'

'Perfection is what we aim for.'

'Do you ever miss the target?'

A corner of his mouth lifted. 'More often than you might think, but we usually manage a cover-up.'

'I find that hard to believe. You have your fingers on all the buttons all the time, by the look of it.'

He was quiet for a moment, then he unlinked his hands and leaned forward, his forearms on the table. 'It's how I live. I'm not comfortable any other way.'

His gaze, deep blue in the dim light, fastened on her, steady and intense. The black wool sweater he wore framed his powerful shoulders and with his arms in that position the sleeves were pulled back a little, revealing his tanned forearms, sprinkled with fine, dark hair.

An intense awareness of him shivered through her.

'Do you ever take a break?'

'Not unless I'm forced to. Tell me,' he said, taking her by surprise, 'about the Amazon.'

Scarlett played for time, slipping out a hand from under the comfort of the throw and picking up her glass. Her teeth nibbled at her bottom lip and she saw his eyes drop to her mouth, his gaze heated and explicit.

'No,' she said softly.

He nodded. 'No,' he agreed. 'Not now.'

'Not ever.'

How much did he already know? Had he looked her up? Most likely, she thought. He'd have done his research. She watched as his fingers gripped the delicate stem of his glass and raised it to his mouth, his eyes returning to hers.

'What do you want to know?' she said after a pause.

'Everything. Except that the jungle is scratchy. I know that already.'

'You haven't been there? Maybe on a cruise up the river?'

He laughed. 'A cruise? I wouldn't last a day before throwing myself to the piranhas. Or worse, throwing someone else to them.'

Scarlett shrugged. The throw slipped, exposing her left shoulder. She glanced down, hoping he wouldn't notice, but she should have remembered he noticed everything. He reached across the small table and lifted the fabric, tucking it around her neck again.

'Thank you,' she said stiffly.

'Soft,' he murmured, 'like your skin.'

She felt heat bloom in her cheeks and her eyelids dropped, as she almost fell victim to the quiet seductiveness of his velvety voice.

Then she straightened her spine, tipping her head back so her hair fell down her back. 'Just one of the touches of luxury with which you indulge your guests,' she retorted. 'Do you like jungles?'

His smile narrowed his eyes, and they crinkled at the corners. She saw that fleeting ghost of a dimple revisit his cheek.

'No. I prefer wide open plains. The savannah. Give me a desert before a jungle, any day.' He looked out into the darkness. 'Although right here is where I always want to be, wherever else I go.'

'I like deserts too.'

'Do you?' He swirled the wine in his glass. Those fingers, she thought, could snap that delicate stem in an instant. 'For someone of your profession, I would have thought a desert is rather lacking.'

'You'd be surprised what can be found growing in a desert, if you know where to look. The Empty Quarter in Arabia…'

'Scarlett—' he interrupted her '—you've changed

the subject. Now, please tell me something else about the Amazon.'

'Okay.' She pulled her feet up and tucked them under the blanket. 'It's dense, hot, steamy. And incredibly noisy. There're squawks, hoots, grunts and rustlings. The sounds, especially at night, are completely alien—totally different from the ones you can hear now, if you listen. The colours are intense. There're blue, red and rare hyacinth macaws in the canopy. You'd never believe there could be that many different shades of green. And the plants...' She stopped and shook her head. 'A few square metres of the forest floor could keep me entranced for hours. There is so much...*so much*...to see and discover.'

That, she thought, was my mistake, although Alan must have been watching and waiting for me to make it. I left the path, and I was too absorbed in the search. She'd been over and over those minutes in her mind, endlessly. Had it been minutes? Or longer? She'd probably never know...

'Go on.'

Will's low voice broke into her thoughts. For a few seconds she was confused, but then his serious face, his eyes intent on hers, came into focus again and she dragged herself back to the present.

'That's what it's like. Why I like...*liked*...being there.'

'And in your search of the forest floor, did you find what you were looking for?'

'It wasn't anything…' But that wasn't true. She— the expedition—had been looking for something very specific. 'We were looking for orchids. Especially one orchid, which was thought to be extinct.'

'Did you find it?'

She shrugged. 'A needle in a haystack would be no challenge at all compared with searching for one small flower in the Amazon rainforest.'

'So that's a no. Will you go back and try again?'

She was quiet for a long time. Then she uncurled her legs from beneath her and put her bare feet on the tiles. She gripped the edges of the throw across her chest.

'I doubt it. This is where I plan to stay now. At Rozendal.'

'Why, Scarlett? Your enthusiasm glows when you talk about plant-hunting. I don't know if Rozendal will ever be worthy of that degree of passion.'

'Oh, it will be. It's my home. Like Bellevale is yours. Would you ever give up your home?'

'Never. But it's been my home for a long time. This is all new to you. It takes years to build up a relationship with a place.' He drained his glass. 'But then it's a relationship that's solid. Trustworthy.'

Scarlett remembered what she'd said—shouted— earlier. 'Yes, I suppose so. I've never had the opportunity to find out until now. But I'm sorry for shouting at you. I think I was just beginning to realise what a huge undertaking the restoration will be. I felt overwhelmed and a little panicky.'

Will rubbed his fingers across his forehead. 'I sensed that, and I'm sorry too. I shouldn't have pushed you like I did.'

'You saw an opportunity to get past my defences and you took it.'

'Yeah. It's how the hard-edged world operates. You have to take your chances and watch your back. It's not what you're familiar with, I'm sure.'

If only you knew, she thought. Those rules applied to everything in life. You had to be on your guard, ready for things to go wrong, so when they did you were prepared. She'd believed her parents when they'd said they'd be back for her in time for the holidays. She hadn't been prepared for that. She'd believed Alan loved her completely, not just for the use he could make of her mind and her research.

She'd believed she'd loved him back.

The only thing left to believe in was herself.

'And the scratches on your arms? Are you going to tell me about that?'

Scarlett clutched at the blanket and stood up. The edge of the soft fabric brushed against her calves. She took a step back from the table, lifting her chin a fraction. 'No,' she replied. 'I'm not.'

Will rose from his chair in a controlled movement. She had a wild and irrational desire to lay her cheek against his chest, to see if his sweater was as soft as it looked. It would be comforting. For a moment she'd feel secure, but it wouldn't last.

'What happened, Scarlett?'

Her throat and mouth were dry, but she couldn't risk reaching for her glass to take a mouthful of wine.

'Nothing that matters.'

'I don't think that's true. I think you're hiding something. Or from someone.' He moved towards her. 'And I think it does matter. Maybe quite a lot.'

He raised a hand and brushed the back of his fingers across her cheek. She turned her head away.

'I'd like you to go now.'

'Wouldn't you like a nightcap? There'll be liqueurs in the minibar. It might help you to sleep.'

'No, thank you. I need to have a clear head in the morning, if I'm going to make a start on Rozendal.'

'Come to my office at ten. Up the steps at the front of the homestead and down the passage on the right. We'll drive over and decide where to begin.'

'I can do that on my own.'

'Yes, you can. But it will be quicker and a lot easier if you let me help you.'

He reached past her and opened the door, stepping back as she walked inside.

He waited until he heard her turn the key in the lock and slide the bolt, before turning away. She was safe, although not from whatever demons were bothering her.

At least she was safe from him.

CHAPTER TWELVE

HE'D SAID SHE should come at ten o'clock, but he'd been pacing the floor since nine-thirty. He'd tried to spend the time usefully, answering emails, but his concentration was fragmented. Lack of sleep normally didn't bother him at all. He could power through on just a couple of hours a night, but perhaps it was catching up with him at last.

Not that he felt like sleeping. He felt like punching something or tackling a triathlon. Anything to release this pent-up frustration and energy which bubbled inside him, making him move restlessly around his office like a caged animal, wearing a track in the carpet. It tugged at his gut and captured his muscles in an unfamiliar grip of tension, and he didn't know how to escape it.

He picked up his phone and scrolled through his contacts. Maybe he should get in touch with that blonde he'd met last month. Dinner and then sex back at her apartment. That would surely afford him at least a few minutes of oblivion.

He dropped the phone onto the desk, swearing under his breath. Nothing felt less appealing. He did not want to wipe the thought of Scarlett from his mind. He wanted to keep her image there. He wanted her in his arms. He was notorious for getting what he wanted. But no matter how much he wanted this, he could not have it. Could not have *her*.

A glance at the antique carriage clock on the mantelpiece told him it was still five minutes to ten. Perhaps the clock wasn't working properly. It tick-tocked steadily, as it had done for more than a hundred years. Why should it slow down now?

His phone vibrated on his desk and he snatched it up, but his frustration ratcheted up another notch as he saw his brother's name light up on the screen. What the hell did he want, and why *now*? He considered rejecting the call, but he knew if he did it would ring again. And again, until he gave in.

'Yeah?'

This conversation was one he'd had many times and would no doubt have to have many times more. He marvelled at how his brother could keep asking. It must be because his wife was standing next to him, telling him what to say. He knew she was because he could hear her voice.

His answer was never going to change. Richard had been quick to accept the deal he'd offered him. Happy to shed his responsibilities. Not that he'd had much choice. It was that or bankruptcy.

He ended the call, tucked the phone into the back pocket of his jeans and ducked his head to scan the grounds through the window. There was still no sign of Scarlett.

'Will?' He swung round, startled even though he was expecting her. That was how frayed his nerves were. 'Is everything okay? If you're busy I could…'

She stood at the door, in snug-fitting jeans and a loose cotton jumper the same green as her eyes. Her braided hair hung over one shoulder and there was a cool box at her feet.

Finally, he understood the meaning of *breathtaking*. The frustration of the past few hours, as he'd waited to see her again, the irritation with his brother, all drained away and he felt something unravel inside him, releasing the knot in his gut. Relief at the sight of her almost made him lightheaded.

'Scarlett. No, I'm not busy. Just a…business call. Come in.'

He wondered how much of his conversation she'd heard. It didn't matter. She'd only have heard his string of refusals. And the expletive with which he'd punctuated the end of the call, as he stabbed at the button.

She didn't move. Her eyes ranged around the room, taking in the pictures on the walls, the antique furniture, the rugs. Her gaze swept over the surface of his desk, with its desktop and laptop computers, beyond to the bookshelves, packed with wine auction catalogues and books on the history of wine-making in the Cape. A slight frown drew her brows together.

He glanced around and saw the room as she might see it. The pale green walls provided a perfect foil for the dark mahogany furniture. The brass which bound the large chest positioned against one wall gleamed with polish, and the richly coloured rugs glowed on the pale wooden floor. A collection of Delft blue and white china filled a glass-fronted cabinet.

It was a beautiful, satisfying room but it was utterly impersonal. That was how he liked it.

The photos on the walls were all of awards given to Bellevale wines, or of staff members celebrating a significant moment of the harvest. One showed a smiling Grace beside a world-famous chef, outside the estate restaurant. The man had given the food a five-star rapturous review and then tried, and failed, to woo Grace away, to work for him.

There were no family photos in silver frames on his desk. No travel souvenirs or childhood mementos.

He wondered if Scarlett would comment.

'You said ten o'clock, I think.' She glanced at the clock as its silvery chime began marking the hour.

Will skirted his desk, exhaling, dropping his shoulders. 'I did. I'm ready to go.'

He'd been ready for hours. He flipped the laptop closed and picked up his car keys.

'I've made a picnic lunch, from the food at the

cottage, so you can just drop me off at Rozendal. I'll be fine...'

'I've cleared my schedule for a few hours. Is there enough for two? If not, I can ask Grace...'

'But you're so busy. I'm sure you don't want to waste any more time.'

'My time is my own, Scarlett. The only person I answer to is me. And you haven't answered my question.'

'That depends on how hungry you are.'

Ravenous, he thought. But no picnic, however lavish, was going to satisfy this particular hunger.

Three hours later, Scarlett sank into one of the ancient lumpy chairs on the veranda of Rozendal and closed her eyes.

Plans, facts and mostly figures filled her brain so that her head buzzed with information, although she felt physically exhausted. The temperature had climbed and at noon, when they'd been at a point furthest from the house, inspecting the old walled garden with its broken glasshouses and storage sheds, it had felt hot. The ancient walls had reflected the heat of the sun, generating warmth which would linger long after the sun had begun its descent towards the west. It would be a perfect place to establish a nursery garden for growing rare plants from seed, if the seed was available. Scarlett made a note to find out.

She'd compiled lists under endless headings on

her phone, cataloguing the basic repairs which needed to be carried out and equipment which had to be replaced.

Most importantly, she'd listed all the plants she could name in the gardens and taken dozens of photographs. Will had promised to lend her a book on the historic flora and fauna of the region. She was looking forward to sitting down later, with a glass of wine at her elbow, when she could begin identifying some of the plants and trees, both native and invasive species, and begin to plan her rewilding strategy.

Will lifted the cool box, put it on the rickety table between the two chairs and sat opposite her.

'Tired?'

'Physically, yes. But my brain is in overdrive. So much to think about.'

'So much to plan.'

They'd dodged around each other all morning. Making sure he didn't touch her had taken a degree of concentration he usually reserved for tasting a new wine or playing a game of poker.

The simple brush of his fingers against hers might cause him to lose it. He couldn't risk that. Another kiss and she'd retreat, refuse to engage with him, and this would all end up taking much longer than necessary.

Time, or the lack of it, was the issue. He had to move the project along as quickly as possible and that meant being with her, helping her. And ultimately persuading her to help him.

He'd discovered she was clever, thoughtful, astute. And she was gorgeous.

His body buzzed with awareness of her: her long, denim-clad legs as she walked in front of him along a narrow path; a glimpse of creamy cleavage as she bent to examine a plant and exclaim over its beauty or unfamiliarity; the fabric of her cotton shirt pulled tight against her perfectly rounded breasts as she stretched up to take a leaf between finger and thumb.

How long could he do this for? A week? Two? Watching her push her fingers into her hair and stretch out her legs made both those estimates seem far-fetched. Right now, his limit was so close he didn't dare to calculate it.

If he reached the end of the day without pulling her into his arms and kissing her until neither of them knew which way was up, he'd consider himself superhuman.

She caught him watching her and he felt another layer of awareness thread through his body. How much had she guessed about the desire that gripped him, dictating his every careful movement?

How much of it did she share?

'What are you thinking about?' The words were out of his mouth before he could stop to consider them.

Scarlett blinked, dark lashes feathering over her cheeks. Across her cheekbones her pale skin was stained with pink.

'That I should have worn a hat?'

'I should have suggested it. The sun…'

'Actually, that wasn't what I was thinking.' She dropped her head against the back of the chair, exposing her smooth throat and neck.

Will swallowed. 'No?'

'No. What was on my mind was something you said yesterday.'

'What was that?' A knot of warning tightened deep inside him. He needed to keep the conversation light and he needed to control it.

'You said I have turned your plans upside down. I think those were your words. What did you mean?'

Will put his glass down. 'Why do you ask? I was simply explaining that your arrival has meant I've had to change my plans. I've done it before. It's possible.'

'Yes, I get that.' Scarlett pushed a tendril of hair off her forehead with the back of a hand. 'I'm just curious to know what huge changes you've ever had to make. From my perspective, you've had an easy life. Your family have owned Bellevale for generations.'

'That's right.' He nodded. 'Centuries. Since they arrived from France, fleeing religious persecution. The date on the main gable of the Belle-vale homestead is 1687.'

'And its succession from one generation to the next has always been smooth, without any major upheavals? A good marriage always made, a son born to inherit?'

'Mostly.'

'Mostly? You see, I can't imagine what that must feel like. Growing up with that certainty, that security, of knowing where you belong, all your life, feels mind-blowing to me. I lost my security when I was sent away to school. I was eight.'

'But then you found your godmother, Margue-rite. You got it back.'

Scarlett smiled, and it made his heart turn over. 'School holidays with Marguerite were interest-ing. Often fun. But I was never secure. I never knew what scheme she would come up with next, or what corner of the country we were going to be dashing off to, on some crazy whim. Some days she forgot about food altogether, so I took to hiding biscuits and pieces of cheese under the mattress. And sometimes she'd disappear, and I wouldn't know when, or even if, she was plan-ning to return.'

She pulled her knees up and wrapped her hands around her shins. 'Sometimes I really did not want another of her adventures. I craved normality and all I wanted to do was lose myself in her over-grown garden. I treasured the time I spent there.

I felt safe. It's where my obsession with plants began.' She leaned forwards, resting her chin on her knees. 'When I arrived for my school holidays, I'd rush straight to the garden to check on the plants. Knowing they'd be there, following the seasons, flowering and setting seed and reappearing in the spring, gave me a sense of continuity and security I couldn't find anywhere else.' She sipped from the glass of lemonade Will had poured for her. 'I'm wondering what blip in your never-ending line of certainty could be called huge?'

Will listened, trying to imagine a childhood where no two days had been the same, when the only certainty had been the changing seasons.

He'd believed Bellevale was home. He knew and loved every inch of the house and the estate, but that wasn't all of it. Like Scarlett, he loved the seasons which came and went with such dependability, year in and year out, whatever was happening around him. He loved the sheltering mountains that enfolded the valley. He loved the animals that roamed the wild places beyond the boundaries, and the birds of prey which soared on the thermals, high above in the endless blue, their haunting calls echoing off the crags.

It was all an intrinsic part of him.

But from a very early age he'd known that, like Scarlett, he hadn't been wanted and that Bellevale would never be his.

That knowledge, which had felt like a shard

of glass embedded in his heart, had forced him to become tough and relentless. Some called his business practices ruthless, but he disputed that. Toughness and determination were what had got him where he was today. Ruthlessness would mean he cared only for himself and that wasn't true. He cared for his staff, deeply, and would do anything to make their lives easier. They returned his care with loyalty and trust, qualities which he valued above all else.

He could not say the same for his family, but that was something he did not discuss, with anyone.

He watched Scarlett as she waited for him to reply and decided to turn the conversation around.

'I can't imagine what your life was like,' he said. 'You lost your ability to trust when your parents deserted you, and your godmother was unreliable, even if she had the best intentions.'

'I suppose you could analyse it like that.'

'And then you found security again, and someone you could trust, but...'

Her green eyes flew wide. 'What do you mean? I haven't said anything about...'

'You haven't needed to.'

Will dropped his eyes to her hands, where they were loosely linked around her legs. A few days of working in the garden, in the autumn sunshine, and that pale band of skin around her finger would fade, erasing all evidence that she'd worn a ring there.

She looked as if every muscle in her body had tensed, primed to flee. He shifted forward in his chair, ready to catch her if she tried to run. That need to keep her safe engulfed him again.

The thumb of her right hand shifted, to rub at the base of her ring finger. 'I…it's nothing. I'm fine with it.'

'Was that what happened in the Amazon, Scarlett? Did he say he'd changed his mind? Ask for the ring back?'

The thought of anyone hurting her made him burn with anger. He'd like to get hold of whoever he was and…

'No,' she replied suddenly, her voice stronger. 'It wasn't like that. Not at all.'

'Then how was it?'

'I gave the ring back. Well, actually, I posted it to him.'

'You broke up with him by *letter*? Not even email or, God forbid, a text? That's so old-fashioned…'

'No letter. Just the ring in an envelope, but I couldn't find one of those padded ones so I wrapped it in a tissue. He didn't need an explanation. He knew what he'd done.'

'What? What had he done, Scarlett?' The need to know felt urgent. 'Had he cheated?'

'No. Not in the way you'd imagine.'

'I don't understand.'

She shrugged her narrow shoulders and twisted round, peering into the picnic box.

'You don't need to. It really doesn't matter now. Would you like a sandwich? Ham or cheese?'

Scarlett walked over to the veranda railing and dusted the crumbs from her hands. A sparrow immediately swooped from the overgrown shrubbery and pecked at them on the gravel below.

She'd avoided Will's questioning, simply by refusing to answer. She'd learned enough about him in the brief time she'd known him to suspect he wouldn't be satisfied with that for long.

'The birdsong this morning was beautiful. I must get a book so I can identify them.'

'I'll lend you one, along with the one about the flora of the Cape I mentioned.' He stood up and packed the remains of the picnic into the box. 'Shall we have a look at the house now?'

She turned as he straightened up, the muscles of his back flexing under the pale blue linen of his shirt. She remembered the smoothness of those muscles beneath her hands, as he'd cupped her head and stroked her collarbone. Had that happened only twenty-four hours ago? The memory felt as if it had always been a part of her: how his back had expanded under her touch as he inhaled, filling his lungs, but then stayed broad as he'd kissed her, not breaking the contact, not even to breathe out.

His long thighs had supported her, steadied her as she'd leaned into him, lost to everything but the exquisite immediate moment.

How could she have forgotten so quickly that those feelings were never meant to last? They were as fragile as spun glass, made to be shattered by the whim of another, just like the trust of a child could be.

The promise she'd made to herself, to banish such feelings from her life, had been swept away the moment Will's mouth had brushed hers and now that memory was bound to her soul. She knew she wouldn't ever be able to shift it.

Will's kiss had felt like nothing that had gone before. The combination of place, circumstances—*him*—had created the perfect storm and she'd been sucked into its peaceful eye where, for a few brief moments, she'd soared, weightless and cherished, while the trauma and chaos of her life had tumbled away.

Luckily, she'd crashed to earth before things had got out of control.

'Yes,' she agreed. 'Let's look at the house. Its condition can't be worse than the gardens and outbuildings.'

But examination of the house proved to be less daunting than she'd anticipated. The roof needed to be rethatched but once the building was watertight and the pigeons and squirrels had been evicted from the loft, redecoration would quickly make a huge difference.

Scarlett followed Will's lead, avoiding floorboards that he decreed unsafe. They peered down the lethal staircase which led to the cellar and closed the door on it.

Scarlett glanced at his grim expression. 'Thank you for saving me from that,' she murmured. 'Even if you gave me a terrible shock in the process.'

'I'm sorry I frightened you. I had to make the decision in a split second.'

Outside, they found a low door beneath the kitchen stoep which gave safer access to the dark semi-underground space.

Huge oak barrels ranged along the walls, a legacy of the time, long gone, when Rozendal had produced wine. Massive beams, festooned with generations of cobwebs, meant Will frequently had to duck his head. It was dry and smelled of ancient wood and dust. Scarlett was relieved to step back into the warm sunshine of the stable yard.

She turned her face to the sun and shivered. 'I don't like it in there. That's not somewhere I'm going to spend much time.'

Will ducked through the door and pulled it closed behind him. He brushed cobwebs from his head.

'You won't need to. It's about the only part of the house that needs no work done on it.'

They returned to the interior, noting holes in skirting boards which mice had probably used on a nightly basis when there'd been food to forage in the kitchen, broken tiles in bathrooms and a broken window under the eaves.

'That's where the haunting bat will have got in.'

'Is the haunting bat related to the ghost bat and the terror bat?'

'Closely,' he said with a smile. 'They all come out at night to prove people wrong who say they're not afraid of them.'

'Hey, I'm not afraid of them. I was tired and confused and I didn't know the thing thumping around my room was a bat. It sounded huge. I've been up close and personal with a *vampire* bat before now.'

'Not too close and personal, I hope.' He lifted the end of her plait and peered at her neck.

Scarlett went very still. Her eyelids dropped and her breathing grew shallow, waiting for the feel of his mouth on her skin. She didn't know what she'd do, but she'd have to stop it, somehow. Her pulse accelerated and she knew he'd see it beating at her throat.

He dropped her plait. 'Can't see anything.' A note like a stretched wire ran through his voice.

'No,' she murmured. 'I didn't let them get *that* close.' She pulled her head away.

Their eyes met, understanding arcing between

them. Scarlett dragged hers away first, turning blindly towards a door and pushing it open.

It was the bedroom where she'd tried to sleep that first night. The daylight through the grimy window showed it up in glaring reality. The bare mattress and ancient pillows were lumpy, and the thin rug was threadbare and moth-eaten.

'This is where I tried to sleep. It's where the haunting bat found me.'

Will stood just inside the door, hands on his hips. 'God, Scarlett, I should never have allowed you to stay here.'

'I was determined.'

'Has anyone ever told you that you're stubborn?'

Scarlett lifted her chin and pushed her hands into the pockets of her jeans.

'I'm not stubborn. I'm strong-minded.'

'There's a difference?'

'Definitely. The first has connotations of unreasonably obstinate behaviour, whereas a strong-minded person is recognised as having a vigorous mind. It's how emancipated women were once described.'

'Presumably by those who disapproved of them, for wanting to separate themselves from a life of drudgery at the kitchen sink?'

Scarlett laughed, and the tension between them faded.

'Probably. Anyway, I don't like being told what to do.'

'I've noticed.' He spoke with feeling, but she saw his mouth lifting at the corners.

They returned to the car in silence but instead of climbing behind the wheel, Will folded his arms and rested them on the top edge of the door, looking up at the old house. Its lines were graceful and pure. Even though chunks of plaster had fallen from the walls and the thatch was green with moss, the classic bones of the structure were undeniable. The date on the tall central gable was no longer legible but it could be discovered and reinstated. He was sure it was only a few years younger than Bellevale.

He wondered what had made his ancestors choose the land they had, rather than this neighbouring piece. He knew it had all originally been one estate and Rozendal had been sold off, either to raise money or reduce the size of Bellevale to make it more manageable.

That made sense, except Rozendal had the water supply which never failed, even during the severest drought. It hadn't been possible to divide that.

By uniting Bellevale and Rozendal he'd simply be reinstating the original boundaries.

He turned to look at Scarlett. She was standing at the edge of the pond which formed the centre of the gravel turning circle. A couple of inches of green, slimy water covered the bottom and long-dead waterlilies drooped from baskets.

'It will be so pretty,' she said, 'when I've fixed it. And I'm going to reinstate the original drive.' She pointed to the place where the two lines of ancient oak trees marched away from them.

He would have described the undergrowth beneath them as impenetrable, but he knew Scarlett had forced her way through it, to burst in on the scene of the auction. No wonder she'd had twigs in her hair and looked wild, but she'd probably thought it easy compared with the Amazon rainforest.

Stubborn, he thought, *associated with unreasonable behaviour.*

'If you do that, you'll have to have the lane leading to the gates cleared and resurfaced too. I don't know how you got that hire car down there. It'd be a challenge for a tank.'

Actually, he did know, because he had gone to look for it yesterday morning. He'd found it parked at a rakish angle and, unbelievably, the keys had still been in the ignition and her cabin baggage in the boot. He'd eyed the tall, rusty gates and wondered how the *hell* she'd managed to climb them, and then he'd taken half an hour to turn the car and bump his way, very slowly, back up the track to the road.

It was well known that in situations of extreme stress the human body, pumped full of adrenalin, could accomplish feats of strength that would normally have been impossible. Scarlett had known the clock was against her, that the auction was happening, and nothing was going to stop her. She'd been desperate not to lose Rozendal.

It was not in the least surprising that she'd crashed so spectacularly afterwards, as soon as she'd known she was safe.

He thought she would have crashed wherever she'd happened to be, but he was glad she'd been in his arms.

They climbed into the car and Will turned to face her.

'I know a builder who'd be perfect for this job.' He nodded towards the house. The sun was lower and the white gables were taking on a softer, buttery glow. 'He owes me a favour.'

Scarlett sighed. 'But that would mean I'd owe you a favour too, Will, and you know I don't want that.'

'Tell me then, how you're going to find someone to do the work.'

'I'll ask around. Grace will…'

'Anyone you ask will tell you to ask me, and I'll recommend this guy. If you use that vigorous mind of yours, you'll see at once that my way will be quicker and better.'

Scarlett leaned back in her seat and folded her arms. 'I don't want…' She turned her head towards him. 'I don't want favours, Will.'

'Now I think you're being stubborn.'

'Will...'

'This man, Peter Langer, is semi-retired and will have the time. I'm not suggesting he does it for a preferential rate. It will be expensive. This kind of specialist restoration work needs to be done with care and sensitivity by someone knowledgeable, like him. He'll also be able to find someone to take on the rethatching. That isn't easy. Shall I call him?'

'Give me his number and I'll call him.'

'Okay. But the first thing he'll do is call me to get the low-down on you, and the job. It'll take longer, and the result will be the same, but the choice is yours.'

'I did tell you that you're bossy, didn't I?'

'Yup, you did. But tell me something new about myself. I already knew that.'

He watched her bite her bottom lip and he thought she was trying not to laugh.

'Hey, you'll hurt your mouth and...'

And then I'll be compelled to kiss you better, carefully but very thoroughly. And all the defences I've spent today building will crumble. Immediately.

'You're bossy, but you're kind too.'

'Kind? Me? If you go around spreading that sort of talk I'll lose my hard man image. I'm ordering you to keep it to yourself.'

'Bossy. *Again.*'

'Difficult to break the habit of a lifetime, even if I wanted to.'

He pressed the ignition switch and eased the big vehicle into gear. He steered around the pond and then stopped at what had been the entrance to the oak-lined driveway.

'How did you do it, Scarlett?'

'How did I do what?'

'How did you fight your way through that jungle, after first climbing the gates? And why did you approach by that route?'

'It's the way the satnav took me. I wasn't in a position to argue with it. Not that time. And I can't remember much about it. Remember I'd been lo… I'd been in the Amazon. My jungle skills were finely honed.' He intercepted her sideways glance. 'And,' she said, 'I'm strong-minded.'

Just how strong-minded she was, Will was beginning to appreciate. He drove her back to Vineyard Cottage and pulled up at the foot of the steps.

'Useful day?'

'Useful, but daunting. How about you? Have you figured out a way to part me from Rozendal yet?'

'Harsh words, Scarlett. I want you to reach your own conclusions about Rozendal. I'm ready to listen when you want to talk.'

He had a sudden, vivid vision of her leaving, broken and defeated, and he hated it. He hadn't expected to enjoy the day but he had, even though he'd spent a lot of time dancing around her, being ultra-cautious. He liked her company and loved it when her guard dropped, letting her sense of humour escape. At least, he thought, he might enjoy the time she was going to spend here. Afterwards, it was unlikely their paths would ever cross again.

For a reason he was unwilling to examine, the idea of never seeing her again felt impossible.

He opened the door, but she raised a hand.

'There's something I'd like to ask you.'

He snapped back to reality, wariness instantly in place. He hadn't answered her earlier question. Was she about to ask it again?

'What?'

'I'll need to see the lawyers in Cape Town, to arrange access to funds. I'll have to make an appointment. Is it an easy city to navigate? I can find my way through uncharted jungle but I'm not so good with the urban kind. Driving in heavy traffic makes me nervous.'

Will drummed his fingers on the steering wheel, setting up a quick rhythm. Scarlett getting to see the lawyers was not going to be difficult. They'd most likely clear their diaries and roll out the red carpet, definitely crack open the sherry, when they knew she was coming to call. Last night he'd looked up Marguerite du Valois. It was startling what you could discover on the internet. Most startling was the information regarding her estimated net worth. He wondered if Scarlett knew just how much of an heiress she was.

'Give them a call in the morning and see how they're fixed,' he said. 'Have you got your phone working?'

Scarlett nodded. 'And my laptop. I found the Wi-Fi instructions.'

'Good. I need to go into Cape Town one day this week, to see our exporters. I could take you.' He needn't mention his intended visit to the company who made hydro-electric components.

'I could drive myself...'

'Yeah, you could.' His fingers resumed their beat on the steering wheel. 'But the freeways are busy, and the driving is nothing like in England. Lane discipline as you know it doesn't exist. And, depending on where you're going, parking can be tricky, if all the pavement space is already taken up.'

'You can park on the *pavement*?'

'You can park anywhere you like. The difficult bit is avoiding the traffic wardens. They take no prisoners.'

'Oh...'

'But I know what a strong-minded and independent woman you are, so...'

'Stop it, Will.'

His fingers stilled. 'Okay. Let me know what they say. I could show you a bit of Cape Town at the same time. I'm a great guide and good company.'

'Really? Who says?'

'Really. And you don't want to know who says.'

He walked round the car to open the door for her and she slid to the ground. Then he followed her up the steps of Vineyard Cottage, stepping back as she unlocked the front door.

'Thanks for today, Will. It was kind of you to be so generous with your time, although I know you also want an excuse to keep an eye on what I'm planning to do.'

'You noticed? I'll have to learn to be more subtle.' But he dropped his head, wanting to hide his expression. It might give away just how much he'd enjoyed being with her and how very hard it was to let her disappear into the cottage and return on his own to the large, empty homestead.

But he'd negotiated the day and he hadn't slipped up. At times the desire to slide his arms around her and feel her pliant body against his, her satiny skin beneath his fingers, her lips under his mouth, had been more powerful than he believed he could resist.

That moment when he'd lifted her hair and studied her neck had been reckless. He'd heard— *seen*—her breathing change, her pulse rate pick up, her pupils dilate. She'd wanted more, just as he had.

But he'd resisted even that.

Move over, Superman. He'd just proved himself to be superhuman.

CHAPTER THIRTEEN

'THEY SAID ANY time is fine.'

Will ran down the steps and turned at the bottom, jogging on the spot. 'I'll collect you at two.'

She watched him disappear along the track, into the trees, plugging his earbuds into his ears, the movement of his arms and legs smooth and coordinated.

She returned to her bedroom and looked at the meagre collection of clothes she'd brought with her. There were jeans, shirts and jumpers. A jacket which, if Will's information about the Cape winter was accurate, was not going to keep her either warm or dry in the months ahead.

The skinny jeans she'd pulled on earlier would do. She swapped yesterday's emerald jumper for a pink one which almost clashed with her hair and slipped her feet into a pair of flat bronze pumps, the only shoes she had packed which were neither walking boots or trainers.

When Will had interrupted her breakfast to ask if she'd spoken to the lawyers she hadn't expected things to move this fast.

'I hope they're reputable.' Now, Scarlett glanced across at him. He hadn't spoken since they'd driven through the gates of Bellevale and he'd lowered his window to call a greeting to a staff member.

There was no hint of the stubble which had roughened his jaw yesterday, so she wouldn't have to try to block the fantasies about how its scrape would feel against her skin. As he'd leaned into the car, pulling the seatbelt out to hand the buckle to her, she'd caught the citrus and sandalwood scent of his cologne, sharp but with underlying notes of smoky sensuality. His hair was damp, towel-dried after a shower, brushed back but curling slightly at the ends, and he'd swapped running shorts and a tee for khaki chinos and a cream linen shirt, top button undone, cuffs rolled back from his wrists.

His straight mouth was set firm. She wondered if he'd even heard her.

Then he flexed his fingers around the wheel and looked sideways at her. 'What makes you say that?'

'The fact that they said I could come and see them any time.'

'So?' Was it her imagination, or did he sound amused? She turned to study his profile again.

'So my point is, they can't be very busy.'

'If it makes you feel better, they are the most prestigious firm of lawyers in the country. They have offices all over the world.'

'Well, I wonder why...'

'Scarlett.' The way he said her name like that— just her name—his voice dropping on the second syllable, did something strange to her insides. It caught her attention and held it. 'Scarlett,' he repeated, 'you're an heiress. They're going to fit you in.'

'I don't like that word. What does it even mean? Anyone who inherits anything is an heir or heiress, even if it's your grandmother's favourite earrings. You were an heir. You inherited Bellevale. It doesn't make you special.'

She saw his jaw tighten and he took one hand off the wheel, pulling his fingers across the back of his head.

'Maybe not,' he said, his eyes fixed on the road as they approached a tight bend. 'But money changes people sometimes, and it also changes how others perceive you.'

'Well, if you perceive that I'm becoming unreasonably demanding, and obsessing over which tree in Italy my olive oil came from, will you tell me? Nip the diva in the bud?'

Will pushed back in the seat, bracing his arms against the wheel. 'Sure.' He sounded amused. 'It'll absolutely be my pleasure.'

Scarlett felt the blush spreading up her neck, over her cheeks. A glance in the wing mirror confirmed that she now had the appearance of a sun blush tomato. She'd walked right into that. She sneaked a look up at him from under her lashes.

The faint comma lines at his mouth had deepened and his eyes sparked.

She went back to studying her hands in her lap. 'I didn't mean...'

'You're blushing. Did I say something to embarrass you?'

'No. I think *I* did.' She raised her head. 'Oh!'

'I wondered when you'd notice. By the end of today you'll have seen it from different angles. I think it's beautiful from all of them.'

In the distance, Table Mountain seemed to rise from the waters of Table Bay, its top hidden under the famous white 'tablecloth' of cloud. It poured like a thick, continuous curtain of candyfloss, disappearing magically at a precise distance from the summit. To the right and left, wrapped in their own ribbons of cloud, stood two lower mountains.

'It's...breathtaking.'

The mountains loomed steadily larger as they sped along the freeway towards the city and soon Scarlett could make out the shimmering steel and glass of towering buildings on the foreshore, green spaces and colourful old houses climbing up the steep streets in cheerful rows.

'Cape Town is in its own mountain amphitheatre, right by the sea. It must be one of the most beautiful cities on earth.'

Will shifted, adjusting his grip on the wheel. The traffic was heavier now, and he braked sharply as a small van cut in front of them.

'Glad you didn't drive yourself?'

'Very. But mainly because I wouldn't have been

able to admire the mountains if I'd been concentrating on the traffic.'

'Mmm.' Will glanced at the satnav screen on the dashboard and indicated left, pulling onto a looping off ramp and entering a maze of busy streets. 'I'll drop you at the door. Send me a message when you're ready to be picked up again.'

CHAPTER FOURTEEN

WILL'S PHONE BUZZED two hours later. When he pulled up at the kerb he saw two men in suits shaking Scarlett's hand. One of them opened the passenger door, nodded to Will and closed it again as she fastened her seatbelt.

'You must have made their day.'

He saw a gap and pulled into the traffic. 'They were very helpful. I had no idea about the money. When I said Marguerite had left me her fortune, I didn't realise it was *a* fortune.'

'How does it feel? Powerful? Exciting?'

'Overwhelming. It'll take time to get used to the idea. But the lawyers have arranged everything. My new bank card arrived by special courier, while I waited. They've suggested making some investments, only they called it "wealth management". I'll have to come back in a couple of days, to sign some papers.'

'Tea? I know a place you'll like.'

'Yes, please. You sound very sure.'

'I am.'

He drove out of the city, the road hugging the curving foot of the mountain.

'Look. Table Bay is behind us and False Bay ahead of us. The flat plain connecting the two was once the seabed, when this peninsula was an island.'

'And on this side the climate is obviously different. It's much greener and there're forests.' Breathless excitement bubbled over in her voice.

'This southern side of the mountain gets almost twice as much rain annually as the city.'

He left the freeway, swooping onto a tree-lined avenue.

Scarlett's response to her first views of the peninsula were joyful and enthusiastic, and he could identify with her feelings. They mirrored his own. Every time he made the journey to Cape Town he marvelled at the spectacular setting, the majestic mountains, the vibrancy of the culture.

They had tea at the Kirstenbosch Botanical Gardens, tucked onto the slopes of Devil's Peak, where the array of indigenous plants and trees fascinated her.

'Did you know there're more than twenty-one thousand plant species in South Africa?' she asked him, looking up from an information board, her eyes lit with passion. 'And many of them are under threat of extinction. They're creating their own seedbank but at the moment seeds are stored at the Millennium Seed Bank run by Kew Gardens, in England.'

'Would you like to see another endangered indigenous species?' Will glanced at the sky. 'There's time for that, and a visit to Cape Point, if we go now.'

They drove towards the wide curve of False Bay, the road climbing and dipping, revealing a new view around every corner. When he pulled into a car park he saw Scarlett's expression of delight as she read the sign.

'Penguins! Is this the famous colony of African penguins?'

He nodded. 'It is. More than two thousand of them. Come on.'

Low slopes covered in coastal bush sheltered the coves below them, where the sea swirled around enormous granite boulders. The waves of False Bay curled onto the sandy beach, each one bringing a group of sleek penguins bodysurfing to the shore.

From the boardwalk which snaked through the bush, they could see the birds and their nests, amongst the roots of the scrub. He watched Scarlett crouch down, intense concentration on her face, as she studied the penguins at close range.

'This is wonderful, Will. Thank you for bringing me here.'

She glowed with enthusiasm and Will wanted to capture her face between his palms and claim her mouth, see her eyes darken with desire. He pushed his hands into his pockets and looked away, wondering why he was submitting himself to the exquisite torture of being close to her when he knew he could not give into his impulse to hold her. He should have collected her from the lawyers' offices and driven her straight back to Bellevale.

Half an hour after leaving the penguin colony at Boulders Beach, Will turned into the Cape Point car park. It was a half mile walk up to the Old Lighthouse at the most south-westerly tip of the African continent, and it was steep, but when they reached the top Scarlett stopped so suddenly that Will cannoned into her. She felt his hands close around her upper arms as he steadied her and she fought the impulse to lean back against the hard expanse of his chest and let him hold her. All afternoon she'd waited for him to touch her hand or sling an arm across her shoulders, but he'd kept his distance and now he dropped his hands as she turned.

'This is amazing!' The steady gale snatched at her words, and he bent his head towards hers. 'Amazing!' she repeated, and he nodded. She stepped towards the stone wall surrounding the base of the lighthouse and leaned into the teeth of the wind.

A fierce gust seized her hair and whipped a strand of it across her face and she lifted a hand to push it away, leaning further out. Far below at the foot of the cliffs the sea churned and boomed, flinging up curtains of spray. She laughed, exuberant, loving the power of the wind and the taste of salt on the air. Suddenly, it felt as if the trauma of her recent past had been swept away, leaving her filled with freedom and excitement.

Anything was possible, with the legacy Marguerite had left her. All her plans and dreams for Rozendal could become reality. She would never have to depend on anyone else again. She let go of her hair and flung her arms out, feeling almost strong and light enough to fly.

'Scarlett!' Will's arms clamped around her waist, pulling her back against his chest.

She turned her head to look up at him, surprised at the anxiety etched on his features. She dropped her hands over his.

'I'm okay, Will.'

She didn't know if he could hear her above the roaring wind and the crashing sea, but he nodded and rested his chin on her head. Then he steered her away from the edge, into the shelter of the lighthouse.

'What were you doing?' he asked when it was possible to speak. 'I thought…' He shook his head. 'I thought you were going to be blown away.'

'I think part of me did blow away.' She turned to face him but he kept his arms around her. 'I'm free, Will. It's starting to sink in, and I feel so strong and powerful, as if I can do anything I want. Because I can, with Marguerite's legacy.' Dizzy with emotion, she rose onto her toes and kissed him quickly before stepping out of the safe circle of his arms. 'You don't need to feel responsible for me any longer.' She reached out a hand and touched his shoulder. 'Hey, I thought you'd be happy about that. I can hire a driver to bring me to Cape Town next time. And I can find someone to advise me about the work at Rozendal.' She smiled up at him. 'Think of all the time and trouble I'm saving you.'

As they set off down the steps, she slipped her hand into his. She glanced up at his austere profile, his wind-whipped hair and straight mouth. Now that she knew her independence was assured and that she'd never have to sell Rozendal, she felt safe with him instead of threatened.

His blue eyes locked with hers and her joyful heart turned over. Doubt nudged at her. Did she really want to find someone else to drive her, or to advise her? Nobody else would be fun to be with, or make her feel safe, like Will did. Enjoying his company, feeling that connection between them didn't mean she was breaking her vow. It wasn't as if she was letting him get close to her or falling in love with him.

She let go of his hand, to prove to herself that she could.

Will negotiated the early evening traffic in silence, reluctant to interrupt Scarlett's thoughts. He supposed she was making a dozen plans which did not involve him and he tried not to let that bother him.

The idea of her being free made him anxious.

He told himself it was because it threw his plans to acquire Rozendal into jeopardy, but he knew the truth was that he wanted her to need him. And with that came the dangerous thought that he was beginning to need her in return.

Was it possible to spend time with her and yet maintain his emotional distance? Allowing himself to admit to an emotional need was unthinkable, and yet with her he felt some of his iron-hard rules softening.

'You're very quiet, Will.'

Her voice startled him. He glanced across at her, noting her expression of concern.

'You're not exactly chatty.' He accelerated past a truck. 'Making plans?'

'Plotting?'

He allowed himself a smile. 'Yeah, plotting how I can convince you that you don't need to hire a driver.'

'How are you getting on with that? Because…'

'I need to be back in Cape Town in a couple of days. If you let me know when your papers are ready to sign, I'll co-ordinate my meeting with yours.'

'Oh…' He thought he detected relief in her voice. 'Because I was going to say I don't really want another driver, if you'll bring me. I…enjoy being with you. I haven't had fun for a long time, but I had fun today, and I hope you enjoyed it too.'

Will felt himself relaxing. He tipped his head back against the seat headrest for a few seconds.

'I love showing newcomers the sights of Cape Town.' He braked before a bend. 'And I... I like being with you.'

'You were right.'

'Aren't I always?'

'No. But this time you were. You're a good guide and great company.'

'We didn't finish the tour today.'

'Perhaps that's a good thing. Any more stunning views and surprising wildlife and I might have started taking it all for granted.'

'I'll make sure that you don't.'

CHAPTER FIFTEEN

'The tablecloth has vanished.'

It was two days later, and Scarlett studied the mountain as they sped along the freeway. The wind had dropped and it was a golden autumn day.

Will nodded, feeling relieved. He'd wanted to show her the mountain without its mantle of cloud. He hoped the day would hold its warmth later on.

He'd collected her from the lawyers' offices and drove them around the base of the mountain, past the university and Kirstenbosch, and Groot Constantia, one of the oldest wine estates in the Cape.

The winding route took them over a dip in the mountain range, which stretched all the way from the city, along the spine of the peninsula to Cape Point, and by late afternoon they were cruising along the spectacular Chapman's Peak Drive, the twisting route carved from the sandstone of the mountainside, swooping down to the stretch of glittering white sand which fringed the beach at Camps Bay.

He pulled into a parking space and they climbed out, leaning against the front of the car. A brisk sea breeze tugged at the loose bun of Scarlett's hair, whipping curls around her face. She laughed.

'Shall we swim?'

'This is the Atlantic. The water is freezing. And I didn't bring swimming things.' He leaned back, resting on the warm metal of the bonnet. 'Did you?'

'Wimp. And no, I didn't.'

'If you want to swim, I can take you to a place in the mountains behind Rozendal. Autumn isn't the best time—it might be chilly—but it's remote, the views are stunning, and we won't have to share it with anyone else.' He scanned the crowded beach. 'None of these people know about it, or they'd be there instead of here.'

'And you wouldn't let them in. You'd stand on the track and repel them all. Single-handed.'

'Bare-handed.'

'Bare-chested.'

'Perhaps we should stop there?'

'Okay.' She swiped the hair from her forehead. 'It's a date, though. A swimming date.'

'A date? I don't date.'

Dating implied thought and possibly planning another meeting. Candlelight and flowers. Those weren't the things on his mind when he scanned the contacts list on his phone.

'An appointment, then. I'm sure you do those.'

From the terrace of the graceful old Mount Nelson Hotel, where they sat sipping cocktails, Scarlett tilted her head to look up at Table Mountain.

'This is perfect.'

Will watched her stir her drink with a striped straw. He'd scarcely been able to keep his eyes off her all afternoon. She was beautiful, with her lustrous green eyes and hair the colour of autumn leaves, threaded through with strands of gold. But her beauty seemed to come from within, a glowing warmth and enthusiasm which he envied.

He remembered the energy with which Scarlett had erupted into Rozendal, robbing him of his victory at the last second, and the determination which had driven her to get there, against all odds. He remembered how the room had buzzed with renewed life, everyone turning to focus on the source of it.

It had been frustrating to have his plans thwarted, but now he wouldn't change it. He wouldn't have missed these times spent with her, watching her relax in his company, her delight in nature and enjoyment of life. He'd get what he wanted, eventually. Having Scarlett as a sparring partner along the way was making the ride far, far more interesting.

Partner. His mind snagged on the word. She'd had a partner. He glanced at her ring finger again. What had happened between them? How could any man have allowed a jewel like Scarlett to slip away? He must have been an idiot. And careless with her. Anger simmered in him at the idea that she'd been hurt.

He stopped, remembering that not everyone,

himself included, needed a partner in life. Perhaps the man had realised his mistake and called it off before it became too messy.

Better a broken engagement than a train smash of a marriage.

'Will? *Will?*'

He dragged his mind back to the present.

'Scarlett.' She stilled, and her teeth scraped over her bottom lip. 'I'm sorry. I was thinking.'

'I could see that. Anything interesting?'

'No.'

'I don't believe you.'

'Sensible. Are you hungry?'

'I will be by the time we get back. Should we leave? It's so perfect here...'

'We could come back another day, if you like.' His mind leapt ahead, racing along a forbidden path. A single call to the concierge would secure one of the grand bedrooms...

But her face clouded and she shook her head. 'I'm going to be much too busy. I shouldn't take any time off. But today has been wonderful.'

'It's not over yet. Today, I mean.'

'I don't know if I can absorb any more beautiful views.'

'That's a pity. I had one more planned.'

'Well, if it really is only one, and it's truly beautiful...'

'You can be the judge.'

He clasped her hand to pull her out of her chair and he didn't let go of it until they reached the car.

They retraced their route, up the steep hill towards Kloof Nek, where the road would tip over the brow of the hill and plunge in a series of bends through the pines, down towards the sea again.

But just before the top Will swung the car to the left.

'Where are we going?'

'To dinner. On the mountain.'

Scarlett leaned forward and looked up. 'In the cable car? Oh, Will…'

'Well, it's a bit late in the day to start walking up, and in those shoes…' He shook his head at her ballet flats.

A stream of vehicles was coming towards them, leaving the lower cable station.

'I think we're too late. Everyone else is leaving. What time does the cable car stop for the night?'

'I have no idea.'

'Oh. We should have skipped the cocktails, or I could have drunk mine more quickly. But it's okay. The view from here is pretty special.'

Will pulled up, leaving the engine running, and took Scarlett's hand to help her from the car. A uniformed man stepped forward.

'Good evening, Mr Duvinage. Enjoy your trip.'

Will nodded. 'Thank you. I'll message you when we're on our way down.'

Scarlett looked up at him, confused, as the stranger drove away in the Range Rover.

'But Will, we don't even know if we're in time...' She turned her head and watched the car disappearing around a bend in the road.

'We don't need the last one, Scarlett. I've booked our own private cable car.'

'You can *do* that?'

'Stop asking questions and I'll show you.'

She took his outstretched hand again.

The ride was spectacular. The floor of the car revolved, giving them a three-sixty view as they ascended, the mountainside quickly dropping away beneath them. Scarlett's knees weakened as they climbed, and she found she was still clutching Will's hand.

She kept her gaze level. At the halfway mark the descending car passed them, packed with noisy trippers on their way down.

'In a few moments, Scarlett...' Will turned his head '...you'll be able to see down to Camps Bay.'

The car swung upwards, seeming to barely clear a jagged ridge of rock, and then the mountain plunged away beneath them, sheer cliffs falling towards the sea.

Scarlett gasped and squeezed her eyes shut.

Will's fingers tightened around her hand.

'Are you okay?'

'Not that good with heights...'

'God, Scarlett, why didn't you say? We didn't have to do this.'

She opened her eyes and found his blue ones, filled with concern, looking down at her.

'I didn't know we were going to do this. And anyway, I wouldn't have missed it…even though it's scary.'

She swayed and Will pulled her against him.

'It's okay. Just a minute to go.'

He put his arm around her shoulders and held her tightly against him. She felt wrapped in safety and put a hand flat against his chest, keeping her eyes fixed on his. The steady beat of his heart thumped beneath her palm and that elusive feeling of belonging—of *fitting*—made her want to stay there in his strong arms, inhaling his scent and feeling the brush of his fingers across her back. Darts of sensation arrowed through her body, meeting at a point in her abdomen, and she pressed herself against him, not caring about letting her feelings show. His hand covered hers and he lifted it, brushing his lips across the tips of her fingers.

The car slowed, inching towards the docking station, swaying slightly. The doors slid open and they stood there for a moment, then Will, keeping an arm around her shoulders, guided her out of the bubble, before slipping several folded notes to the operator.

'Thank you, sir.' The man raised a hand. 'See you later. Whenever you're ready.'

Dusk, thought Scarlett. The perfect word to describe the softly fading light. She looked up into the deep sky and turned in a circle. It was quiet, high above the sounds of the city. Far below, lights had begun to flicker on, spreading a jewelled net over the darkening streets and buildings.

On the western side, the sun was poised above the ocean, its rim seeming to test the water before committing to a swim. The sky flushed orange, pink and then lilac as it sank, spreading the last of its rays over the dark blue and silver of the sea.

'Are you ready for dinner?'

'I think we're too late. The café is closed.'

He smiled. 'Come this way.'

A gazebo, housing a table and two chairs, had been set up, facing the view. Candlelight glowed in glass lanterns and a picnic hamper stood open on the ground. Each chair had a woollen rug folded over the backrest.

Scarlett stopped, a hand going to her heart.

'How did you do this, Will?'

He shrugged. 'I made some calls.'

Will placed a hand on the small of her back and urged her towards the table, pulling out a chair for her. Then he released the ties on three sides of the structure, letting the canvas roll down to protect them from the cool breeze, but leaving the side facing the view open.

He pulled a bottle of local sparkling wine from a cooler and eased the cork from the neck with sure fingers. Honey-gold bubbles fizzed into delicate flutes and he raised his towards her.

'To the heiress.'

'If this is the life an heiress leads, perhaps I could get used to it.' Scarlett sipped. 'Do you live like this all the time?'

'Not *all* the time, no.'

'When you inherited Bellevale did you celebrate like this?'

Will thought back to the day when Bellevale had finally become his. There'd been no champagne opened, no toasts drunk, just a sense of having finally achieved what he'd been striving for since he'd been a boy. It had been a bitter process.

In the confines of this tent, enveloped in Scarlett's burgeoning acceptance of her new status, he felt uneasy. He hated talking about his past, but he didn't like that she had a skewed perception of him. If he tried to explain how he'd come to be the man he was today, would she begin to understand what drove him? Why, when he'd set his mind on something, he couldn't rest until he'd achieved it?

'Will? I'm sorry. Obviously, you didn't celebrate, because your father must have died when you took over Bellevale.'

'Scarlett.' She stopped, her eyes fastening onto

his. 'Scarlett, my parents are still alive. I didn't inherit Bellevale. I bought it.'

Her mouth opened and all he could think was that he wanted to kiss her.

'You…*bought*… Bellevale? But you're a Duvinage. Your family have owned the estate since…'

'1687.'

'Yes. I'm sure you can see why I'm confused.'

'Of course. Why wouldn't you be? Your logic is faultless.'

Will gripped his hands together and looked out into the darkness, wondering why he'd thought starting this conversation was a good idea. He'd made it known to his friends and associates that this was something he would not discuss, under any circumstances. His family didn't count. He discussed nothing with them, anyway.

Nothing about the past could be changed. The subject stirred up feelings of bitter resentment, animosity and, he had to admit, although he wasn't proud of it, an empty sort of triumph.

It was best kept under the carpet, where he'd insisted on sweeping it. Only now he'd lifted a corner…

'Will? I'm sorry. I can see this is difficult for you. If you'd rather not talk about it, I understand.'

It was her empathy which made him want to carry on. She wasn't pushing him for details. He knew he could let the subject drop, if he wanted, and she *would* understand. It felt safe.

'Like you, Scarlett, I was a surprise: the unwelcome and unwanted baby.'

Shock showed in her wide eyes and the small frown between her brows.

'But your parents must have wanted an heir...'

He nodded. 'Oh, yes, they wanted an heir to take over Bellevale. But only one. They weren't—*aren't*—invested in family. "One and done" was their plan, and they had my brother.'

'But if they already had a son, why...?'

'Why did they have me? They never intended to, but I came along anyway.'

'So it was your brother...'

'Richard.'

'It was your older brother, Richard, who took over Bellevale.'

Scarlett reached out a hand towards him. He'd held it many times that day, but now he let her hand, with the pale stripe around the ring finger, lie unclaimed on the linen tablecloth.

'You got that in one.'

'Don't, Will. Don't do that.'

'What?'

'It's not a joke.'

'People joked that I had the passion for Bellevale but it wouldn't be mine, while Richard... All it achieved was to make me determined that I would, ultimately, own it.'

Scarlett withdrew her hand. 'Do you want to tell me what happened?'

Will pulled a hand across his face and took in a long breath.

'Long story short. Richard was raised to run the estate. He was told from day one where his future lay.'

'And you?'

'I was told my future lay anywhere but at Belle-vale. There was room for one owner and that wasn't ever going to be me. I can see that the way our parents handled it resulted in an outcome precisely opposite from the one they intended.' He shook his head. 'Richard was never given a choice and he rebelled against the restriction. Everything my parents did was directed towards his future ownership. It was understood that I would leave and stay out of the way.'

'Did you rebel against that?'

'I suppose I did, in a different way. Richard became a sulky teenager, resentful of being expected to learn about viticulture and oenology, while I was hell-bent on learning as much as I could. I also had to make enough money to buy him out one day.'

'And you did.'

'I did a maths degree and joined a software company in the States. Then I saw a gap in the market for a piece of software. It was such an obvious thing, which is probably why everyone else had dismissed it as irrelevant. I raced to develop it, and it was so successful I was able to start my own company. And then, as happens, I was taken over by one of the giants. Suddenly I had billions and there was only one thing I wanted to spend them on.'

'You're a tech billionaire. Did you make him a hugely inflated offer?'

'Considering the condition the estate was in by then, my offer was generous. Our father had retired and Richard had let everything slide. He simply didn't possess the interest or drive to keep up the momentum which running something like a vineyard requires. It's not easy. Farming is precarious, dependent on so many variables. Droughts are more common than they used to be and there is so much more pressure on water supplies, with the increase in numbers of people living in the Western Cape.'

Scarlett nodded, her lips and cheekbones highlighted in the glow of the candles, her eyes forest green. 'It's a beautiful environment.'

'The rainfall is unreliable, and the one thing everyone needs is water.'

'And your brother wanted out.'

Will chewed his lip. 'I…suggested to him that he might be happier living a different life. Bellevale is isolated. He spent a lot of time driving to and from Cape Town, socialising. Being on his own doesn't suit him.'

'Perhaps if he'd had a partner, it might have been different.'

'Maybe, but he didn't. He, with our parents encouraging him, asked for more money. I upped the offer several times, but they knew what I was worth, and how much I wanted the estate. They'd always known I loved it, so they kept pushing. Eventually I paid him an obscene amount, but I made the conditions very clear. There would be no more money and they—all of them—were to stay away from me and from Bellevale.'

'You don't ever see them? Talk to them?'

'Oh, I do. He still asks for more, quite regularly. He grew up believing the world, or rather Bellevale, owed him a living. He has never understood the concept of earning it.'

'I'm sorry, Will. I've wished I had a family: parents who cared; a sibling who understood. It's lonely without someone to share everyday life with. I think that's why I...' She shook her head, reaching towards him again, and this time he closed his fingers around hers.

'Why you did what, Scarlett?'

'It doesn't matter. This isn't about me.'

'This is about you. I wouldn't have arranged it for myself.' *Or anyone else.* He looked at his watch, angling his wrist to read the time by the light of the candle. 'I think we'd better call for our glass coach and get back down the mountain.'

'It'd be tricky if it turned into a pumpkin.'

'And you ran away...'

'And lost a shoe...'

'Like I said, *those shoes*.'

He stood, picking up the rug from his chair and shaking it out before tucking it around Scarlett's shoulders.

'Surely we should leave the rugs with the picnic things?'

He allowed his hands to rest on her shoulders. 'I'll make sure this one is returned to the restaurant tomorrow. You need it now. The temperature has dropped.'

She turned to face him, holding both his hands. 'Could we stay a little longer? It's not midnight yet…'

He bent his head and rested his forehead against hers. 'It's not, and I'd love to stay longer, but the cable car operator will need to get home, as well as the car park attendant.' He kissed her temple and she shivered. 'And you're cold.'

'That wasn't a cold shiver. It was a…'

He pressed a finger to her lips. 'Shh, sweetheart.'

He pulled out his phone and sent a message, then used the phone flashlight to light their way over the rough ground. Their arms bumped together as they walked side by side to the cable station.

'Going down will be less scary because you won't be able to see how far away the ground is.'

Scarlett laughed. 'My imagination will make it far worse than it is.'

Will took her hand as they stepped into the dimly lit car. 'Imagine you're Cinderella and the worst thing that can happen is that your glass coach turns into a pumpkin.'

'That *is* the worst that could happen. It'd be catastrophic. Suspended from a cable at three and a half thousand feet? In a pumpkin.'

He laughed. 'As you said, it's not midnight yet so I think we'll be okay. But I'll call for the Range Rover, just so we're prepared.'

The driver had the car waiting for them, engine running, when they stepped out of the lower cable station.

'Still think the view is special from here?' Will spun the wheel and pulled onto the road.

'Mmm.' Scarlett snuggled into the folds of the blanket, her head turned towards him. 'Yes. And the view of Cape Town is stunning too.'

'Scarlett. Are you flirting with me?'

'Possibly.'

'I thought so.'

He kept his eyes on the road, the headlights slicing through the dark. *Home*. Her use of the word made him feel good, until he remembered he wanted to part her from her home, or a piece of it. He exhaled deliberately, trying to focus his thoughts on the day they'd spent together, and not on a future in which they'd clash.

She was so still that he thought she'd gone to sleep. He glanced across at her, lifted a hand off the steering wheel and tucked the blanket around her more securely.

'Will?'

'Sorry. Did I wake you?'

'No. Do you regret telling me about your family?'

'I try not to regret things. It's a waste of energy.'

'But what if you really, really wish something hadn't happened? And it's hard to stop the wishing?'

He thought for a while. Did she wish she'd never been engaged, or had a relationship with the idiot who'd broken her heart? Or did she wish she was still with him, her heart intact?

He needed to know the answer.

'Perhaps if you learn from the thing that happened you won't let something like that happen again.'

'If only I could believe I'd learned. And Will?'

'Mmm?'

'That blip which disturbed the line of inheritance of Bellevale was significant.'

'Yeah. It was notable.'

'I'm sorry about the things I said that day in the rose garden.'

'That's okay. You made the obvious assumption.'

He hadn't told her everything. What he'd kept hidden made him feel ashamed and betrayed. It had upended his life and the scandal had played out in the glare of publicity.

But he'd learned never to make *that* mistake again.

Thinking about it made him want to punch something. *Someone.*

The throb of the engine died into perfect silence. Vineyard Cottage was shrouded in darkness, although he knew a motion detector light would come on at the front door.

He listened to the quiet for a minute, unwilling to end it—to break the spell.

Scarlett slept in the passenger seat, her cheek cupped in one hand. Will opened her door and carefully stretched across her to release the seatbelt buckle.

He shook her shoulder gently. 'Scarlett. We're home.' He smoothed a lock of hair back from her forehead. 'You need to wake up so you can go back to sleep in your own bed.'

The urge to kiss her was almost more than he could resist. He lifted his hands and gripped the edge of the roof of the car. Her lids fluttered and he saw the confusion in her eyes, and then clarity dawning as she focused on him.

'Thank you, Will, for such a fun day.' She pushed herself upright. 'But I'll need to edit my TripAdvisor review.'

He tried to release his clenched jaw so he could reply.

'What do you mean?' A whisper was all he could manage.

'You're a great guide and *very* good company.'

'I am?'

'Mmm.'

She reached out her hand and touched his cheek, but he circled her wrist with a finger and thumb and moved her hand away.

'Come on. Bed.'

'With you?'

She slid to the ground and he put a hand on her back, guiding her towards the steps. The light came on and she blinked.

'You're flirting again, Scarlett.'

'Just asking a question.'

As she stepped onto the bottom step, he brushed his mouth over her temple.

'Goodnight, Scarlett.'

He left the car on the drive and took the steps two at a time. The familiar smell of leather and beeswax polish hit him as he pushed open the dining room door and crossed the floor to the drinks cabinet. As the amber whisky swirled into the heavy tumbler gripped in his hand he sniffed deeply, hoping the peaty smell would drive Scarlett's scent from his memory.

He eyed the bottle. How much more of its contents would he need to drink before sweet oblivion overcame him?

* * *

Scarlett pushed the door closed behind her and leaned against it, pressing her palms against the cool wood. She breathed slowly, trying to regulate her heartbeat. If she'd repeated her question, would he have followed her in?

She didn't know. What she knew was that she'd wanted him to. Her heart broke for him. She wanted to hold him, comfort him, tell him how amazing he was. And she wanted to experience that sense of safety and belonging again. She thought it could become necessary to her, as fundamental as air and water.

Perhaps she should be grateful that he'd shown more willpower than she had.

CHAPTER SIXTEEN

SHE HADN'T SEEN Will for over a week.

He'd vanished from her life, but he'd put several things in motion towards the renovation of Rozendal, without asking her.

The morning after their magical dinner on Table Mountain, Peter, the builder, had knocked on her door, at his shoulder a man who could rethatch the house and outbuildings.

She'd asked for contracts to sign but they'd shrugged their shoulders. They'd worked for Will for years, they said. His word was good enough.

'You're working for me,' she'd replied acidly, and they'd laughed and left.

After that, everything moved quickly.

Scaffolding went up around Rozendal. A huge tarpaulin shrouded the roof.

'Just in case the winter rains come early,' Jonas, the thatcher, said, looking skywards.

Peter had a man for everything. A plumber restored the water supply so the water ran clear and smooth, the noisy hiccoughs cleared from the pipes. An electrician frowned and sucked his teeth over the fuse box and muttered about rewiring the entire house, but made it work, anyway.

Scarlett needed it to be weather-proof for the

coming winter, with a functioning kitchen and bathroom and a bedroom where she could sleep in a warm, comfortable bed. And she had to be out of Vineyard Cottage in a week.

Everything else could wait for the spring.

Then, early one morning, she looked up from polishing the bronze kitchen taps and Will was standing in the doorway, leaning a shoulder into the frame.

It was eight days since she'd seen him, not that she was counting.

He pushed away from the door and stepped over the threshold.

Scarlett dropped the polishing cloth into the sink and wiped her hands down her jeans.

'Will.'

'I've been away. Board meetings in Johannesburg and Cape Town.' He leaned across her and twisted one of the taps. A stream of clear water ran smoothly into the sink. 'No more rusty water.'

A mix of emotions chased through Scarlett. She felt a little flare of pleasure, knowing he'd been away, not simply avoiding her. She took a steadying breath, filling her lungs and exhaling slowly. This was Will, and they'd had a beautiful afternoon and then, two days later, an enchanting evening in Cape Town. He'd gone away without telling her. Big deal. Huge. She told herself to get a grip. He did not have to tell her anything.

So why was her heartbeat ignoring her stern inner voice and beating to an entirely inappropriate rhythm? She remembered, uncomfortably, how she'd brushed her fingers across his cheek and he'd gently removed her hand, the gesture speaking louder than any words could have done. And she'd nonetheless half suggested that he come to bed with her. She felt heat flare across her cheeks.

His navy-blue eyes skimmed her face and settled on her mouth for longer than they should have. Her pulse leapt again as she swiped the tip of her tongue across her lower lip.

One corner of his mouth lifted a fraction and his gaze shifted to lock with hers.

'How's the rewilding project coming on?'

Scarlett looked out over the neglected gardens and fields, to the towering mountains beyond.

'I've been in touch with the Seed Collections Officer at Kirstenbosch and he's keen to help. Everyone has been enthusiastic.' She pushed herself upright. 'Except you.'

'Mmm.'

'Have you come to check on progress?'

'No. I've come to make an appointment with you.' He turned and leaned his hips against the worktop, pushing his hands into his pockets. 'A swimming appointment.'

'Oh… I thought you'd forgotten…'

'Scarlett.' She wrapped her arms across her

waist, allowing his soft pronunciation of her name to settle over her. 'Why would I forget?'

It felt as if a chasm had opened up between them: between the relaxed easiness of the days they'd spent together and now. Had Will used the time away to withdraw from her? Had her half-joking invitation made him cautious? That was how it seemed. And Scarlett felt tongue-tied and awkward, as if they were strangers striking up a conversation on a station platform.

'No, of course you wouldn't forget. But if you've changed your mind you don't have to…'

'I'm not known for changing my mind, Scarlett. But if you've changed yours…'

'No! No, I haven't.' She stumbled over her words. 'I'd love to go swimming, only you said autumn wasn't the best time and…'

Then she remembered how she'd stepped out of Vineyard Cottage that morning and been shocked by the temperature. A hot, unsettling breeze had whipped her hair across her face, and the air smelled of dust.

'A day like today is perfect for swimming. There's a berg wind blowing. It's the hot, dry wind which comes down from the high escarpment in the interior. By tomorrow it could be twenty degrees cooler, with mist and rain.'

Scarlett looked out at the sky, its blueness dulled by the dusty air. It was hard to believe it might rain soon and grow cold.

She knew Will's eyes were on her while he waited for her answer. It would be difficult to come up with a reason why she didn't want to go swimming. And anyway, she did. She just wasn't sure she *should*.

'Scarlett?'

'Yes. I mean, *yes*?' She pressed a palm to her forehead.

'Hey.' His voice gentled. 'Even if you don't want to swim, I'd like to show you the place.'

The track twisted up the slope behind Rozendal, through outcrops of grey boulders and clumps of pine trees. The air was thick and warm in her throat and lungs.

'After the cooler temperatures of the past week this feels unnatural.'

'Yeah.' Will settled into a steady pace, just ahead of her. 'It only ever lasts a day.'

The pool lay in a basin of rock. Shelves of sandstone surrounded the clear water and smooth pebbles lined the bottom. Water tumbled down the mountainside beyond and over a lip of rock, creating a gentle splash, and near to where Scarlett stood beside Will it overflowed over a much higher cliff, plunging onto rocks far below before gathering itself to flow in an even stream through the valley.

Scarlett spread her arms wide. 'This is the most

perfect place.' She pushed her fingers through her hair, fanning it out over her shoulders. 'Better than any beach.'

'The Rozendal boundary lies just above the waterfall.' Will extended an arm to show her. 'This is your pool. And that's the river which flows along the edge of your estate.'

'It's beautiful.' Scarlett sent a silent message to Marguerite, as she did every day, thanking her for rescuing her when she'd most needed it, and for delivering her to this place. 'I feel so…lucky.'

Will bent to untie his boots. 'Time to cool off.'

'And no crowds at all.'

'I said I'd fight them off.'

'Bare-handed.'

'Bare-chested, I think you said.'

'You said we should stop there…'

Will began to undo the buttons of his shirt. His teasing gaze held Scarlett's anxious one.

'Wimp?'

'Not fair. I was referring to the cold water. Not…'

'Not what, Scarlett?'

If her cheeks hadn't already been flushed from the exertion of the hike, she knew they'd be burning now. She clamped her arms across her chest.

'Not being afraid of seeing you strip your clothes off. And I'm not.'

Will peeled off his shirt and she felt her stomach lurch. His shoulders gleamed, smooth and golden in the sun, while his sculpted chest and abs tapered to slim hips. A dusting of dark hair narrowed to a line which disappeared, tantalisingly, beneath the waistband of his jeans.

As if her gaze had some sort of power, his fingers popped the button and he pushed the jeans over his hips.

'God, Will…' She turned away.

'It's okay, Scarlett.' There was laughter in his voice. 'I'm wearing shorts underneath.'

Scarlett risked a glance over her shoulder, in time to see him stretch his arms skywards and dive in a clean arc from the rock platform, slicing into the crystalline water.

He surfaced near the edge, tossing his hair from his eyes and scattering a bright shower of droplets over her. The spatter of water was deliciously cool on her skin.

'Are you coming in?'

'I…don't know.'

'You said you were going to change into swimming things.'

'I did.' The blinding truth, that it would have been way safer to swim with Will at a crowded beach than alone in a wild pool high in the mountains, hit Scarlett. 'But I'm not sure…'

He swam to the edge and rested his folded arms on the rock, looking up at her.

'What aren't you sure about? It's perfectly safe. No sharks. No piranhas.'

Just you, she thought desperately. 'It's not that...'

Too late, she saw his arm stretch out and felt his fingers circle her ankle.

'Come on, Scarlett. It might be your only chance. You can't say you went to South Africa and didn't go swimming.' His touch was light, but she felt the stroke of his thumb on her inner anklebone. Who knew the anklebone was such a sensitive spot? A hot current of sensation zipped up her leg.

Piranhas. His words cut through the confusion which clouded her brain, jolting her back to reality. He was so sure of himself, she thought. So determined that he'd get Rozendal, and she knew he wouldn't care what happened to her, once he'd got what he wanted. She'd been stupid to allow the romanticism of a candlelit picnic skew her judgement.

Were all men the same, or had she been unlucky to meet two similar ones in quick succession?

She wasn't going anywhere, except maybe into this water. A hot gust of wind ruffled the surface and scorched her skin. She really, really wanted to swim. His body made her want to run her hands over him and drive him wild and his eyes were daring her to do exactly that. None of that was going to happen. His reaction to her touch, late that night, had been decisive. Was he testing her, to see if he could provoke her to do it again? Playing with her emotions?

'If you'll let go of my ankle, Will, I'll come in.'

He released her and pushed himself away from the side, floating on his back, kicking out into the middle of the pool.

Scarlett turned and pulled off her boots, jeans and shirt, fumbling with the buttons in her haste. For a second, she wished she'd worn a black one-piece swimsuit and not a purple bikini, but she pushed the thought away, refusing to allow herself to be intimidated.

Over her shoulder she could see that Will was still floating on his back, his eyes closed. She stepped to the edge and slid into the silky water.

The icy temperature was so unexpected that she gasped.

Will rolled over onto his stomach and dived beneath the surface. She watched him swim towards her, underwater.

He surfaced close to where Scarlett was suspended in the water, one hand gripping the ledge of rock. Goosebumps roughened her skin and she shuddered.

'You didn't say it was cold.'

'It's water off the mountain, Scarlett. It's always cold.' He sluiced water from his hair. 'Swim a bit. You'll warm up if you move.'

Scarlett released her grip on the rock and he watched her swim with long, steady strokes across the pool. He caught up with her as she reached the waterfall. Ducking beneath the curtain of water, he emerged in the space behind it.

'Will?'

'Come in here. It's…'

She appeared next to him in a shower of bubbles and droplets. Her hair, darkened to the colour of polished mahogany by the water, floated behind her. The emerald of her eyes was intensified by the greenish light reflected off the shadowed water. Close up, he could see a new, faint sprinkling of freckles across the bridge of her nose.

'This is beautiful.' She looked up. Moss and ferns grew on the underside of the lip of rock. Another shade of green, he thought. 'Have you always swum here?'

Will nodded. 'We came here all the time as kids. Whoever was living at Rozendal never seemed to mind.'

He wondered what the hell he'd been thinking, encouraging her into the water with him, and then, even worse, bringing her into this secret place behind the waterfall. It was closed off from the outside world—cool and quiet and…*intimate*. The word beat repeatedly in his brain. This was all kinds of crazy, but when he was around her he felt as if his compass swung out of control. Scarlett became his true north.

He'd stayed away longer than necessary. She'd become almost irresistible, that afternoon in Cape Town, and it had taken all his willpower not to follow her into Vineyard Cottage that night. The pull she exercised over him was unfamiliar and therefore not to be trusted. It was outside the parameters of his experience, and he dared not explore it.

A week should have been long enough, but he could see now that no measure of time away from her would be sufficient to snap this thread that pulled them together. With her, he behaved in a way he didn't recognise. He should have been cool and distant this morning. If he gave into this temptation—this *need*—which had invaded his mind and body, leaving space for nothing but thoughts of how she'd feel in his arms, under him, the barriers he'd built to keep himself safe would crumble.

He couldn't face that. He'd be vulnerable again, in a way he'd only ever been once in his life. The thought was terrifying.

'Will?' Her voice was puzzled. 'Are you okay?'

He shook his head to clear his thoughts, trying to focus on something other than her toned limbs moving in the water, the purple bikini covering, but not concealing much, her body taut with the cold, her rounded breasts peaked beneath the silky fabric.

'Yeah.' His voice felt as if he'd swallowed sandpaper. He wished he hadn't mentioned piranhas. It had made her drop that shutter he'd seen before, when he'd tried to talk to her about the expedition to the Amazon, and he hated that he'd triggered a bad memory for her. 'Just thinking that you're cold. Maybe we should get some sun to warm us up.'

And get us out of here.

She shuddered as a spasm of shivering shook her, turning herself in the water. 'Okay.'

As she moved, her fingers trailed across his chest. He felt the light rake of her nails and his mind blanked. She kicked away but her legs tangled with his as he did the same and suddenly they were face to face, skin to skin, behind the waterfall.

Will felt himself going into freefall and there was nothing he could do to stop it—nothing he *wanted* to do. He slid an arm around her waist to steady her and ran his other hand over her hair, pressing it away from her forehead, his palm coming to rest on the side of her neck. His thumb stroked along her collarbone as his fingers curled over her smooth shoulder.

Her hands rested on his chest and he waited for her to push him away. When she didn't, he pulled her towards him, holding her gently enough so that she could resist if she wanted to. But her hands moved from his chest, round to his back, and he felt her palms pressing against his shoulder blades.

'Scarlett.' It was almost a groan, as if all the forbidden emotion he'd kept tightly coiled inside him for ever was being released at once.

'Mmm?'

He thought he might drown, not in the water but in the depths of her eyes, and in the wave of desire, pure and focused, which crashed over him.

Her breath feathered across his cheek, and he found her mouth. Despite the cold, her lips were warm and soft, and he held back, tasting her, licking the drops of water from her skin before returning to the kiss.

They'd kissed before and he had a vivid memory of how he'd wanted it to go on for ever. This was on another level. There was no space for wondering if it would end. Time ceased to have any meaning at all.

He'd wanted this, dreamed about it, knowing that having it would leave him on the edge of self-destruction, but now that it was happening all his instincts for self-preservation had evaporated. He clung to his self-control, desperate to have more of her but afraid of taking too much, too soon. He brushed her bottom lip with the tip of his tongue, nipped at it with his teeth and he felt her shudder and her mouth open.

Still he resisted, knowing that once he'd crossed that line all other lines would blur. Her back arched and her aroused body scraped against his chest. One of his hands drifted around her waist and came to rest on her ribs, beneath the swell of her breast, his thumb perilously close to its peak.

Then she went rigid in his arms and suddenly

there was cold space between them, her hands on his shoulders, her mouth dragged away from his.

'Will, no!'

This time, he didn't know how he'd be able to stop. Scarlett was pulling away from him, shaking her head. He'd promised himself he'd let her go if she resisted him, but instinctively he felt himself trying to hold onto her. His body clamoured for more. His drugged brain was being slow to catch up.

'Scarlett. Please…'

Her fingers gripped his biceps and then went to where his hands spanned her ribcage. She unpeeled his fingers but wrapped his hands in hers.

'I'm sorry, Will…'

'No.' He finally managed a coherent thought, dragging words up from somewhere. 'I didn't mean this to happen.' He pulled in a breath, trying to find oxygen. 'Please don't apologise.'

'I'm sorry,' she said again, her teeth beginning to chatter. 'I just…can't.'

He swam alongside her to the edge. When he put his hands on her waist to help her out of the water she didn't protest. He stayed submerged for a few more minutes, trying to get his thoughts into some sort of order, and his ragged breathing under control. He felt as if he'd tried to run a marathon and not made it to the end. He'd fought a battle with himself and lost.

His mind, so trained to control his environment, had failed to control his body.

Scarlett sat with her back against a rock, in a place sheltered from the wind. She wore an expression of fierce concentration as she squeezed water from her hair. She did not look up as he sat down a safe distance from her, leaning back on his hands and stretching out his legs.

There was no way he could pretend it hadn't happened. They both needed to acknowledge this thing which burned between them.

Every cell in his body wanted her—wanted to hold her, kiss her, make love to her. But what if he found that wasn't enough? He couldn't risk that.

She wanted him, of that he was sure, but something stopped her.

Perhaps he should be grateful for whatever it was.

She looked up at last, and their eyes collided. She chewed her bottom lip and bent her legs up, hugging her knees to her chest. Was she trying to ensure there was less of her to see, or was it an unconscious gesture of self-protection?

'Scarlett…'

'Will.' She held up a hand, palm flattened towards him. 'You don't need to say anything.'

'You want me.' Those weren't the words he'd planned to say, but they were the ones hammering in his head. Her eyes flew wide and she opened her mouth to speak, but he interrupted her. 'Don't deny it. If you choose not to act on it, that's fine, but just don't...*deny* it.' He rubbed his forehead, fighting to keep his voice steady. 'Because that would be a lie.'

He thought she'd be angry, perhaps walk away, but she dipped her head and linked her fingers around her shins.

'Yes,' she said, her voice quiet. 'I want you. So much it's almost...too much to manage. But like I said—' she glanced across the pool towards the waterfall '—I just...can't.'

'Can't, or don't choose to?' He shook his head. 'You suggested I might come to bed with you.'

'I wanted you to, but you were right to refuse. I'm not in a good place.'

The droplets of water on her skin were drying quickly but a trickle still dripped from the ends of her hair across her shoulders. His eyes were drawn to the slight movement as her hands tightened their interlaced grip, just below her knees.

The band of paler skin around her finger had almost disappeared and a piece of the puzzle that was Scarlett clicked into place in his brain.

'What happened, Scarlett?' He kept his voice even and low. 'What did he do to you?'

CHAPTER SEVENTEEN

SCARLETT SQUEEZED HER eyes shut and shook her head. 'You don't need to know.'

'Maybe not. But I'd like you to tell me.' Will bent his legs and propped his forearms on his knees. 'Sometimes talking can help.'

There was bitterness in her quiet laugh. 'Says the man who doesn't talk to his family. Have you ever thought it might help you?'

'I drove what happened between my brother, my parents and me. There is nothing to discuss. But it sounds as if whatever happened to you in the Amazon was out of your control.'

She didn't answer. He was right and she was sure he knew it. She tried to suppress the rising sense of panic she felt, if she allowed her mind to travel back to that place.

'Have you talked to anyone?'

She breathed in, counting, and then out again. Not panicking had kept her alive. She could deal with this.

'No. I haven't. There wasn't anyone…' Her voice wobbled.

'Scarlett.'

It was the way he had of saying her name. It

soothed her like a balm, made her relax, and relaxing her guard was the worst thing...

Too late, she felt tears clogging her throat, stinging her eyes. She squeezed her lids together but the scalding tears spilled onto her cheeks.

She scrubbed at them angrily with the heels of her hands, biting her lip to stop it from quivering.

'This is so stupid. I don't cry...'

She didn't hear him move but she felt him beside her. His arm was gentle around her shoulders as he pulled her against him, cradling her head onto his chest. She tried to curl into a ball, but he kept her there, wrapping his legs around her, trapping her between his thighs.

'Scarlett, sweetheart, talk to me. Tell me what happened.'

'I'm sorry...'

'If you apologise again, I may get impatient.'

'I'm saying sorry for crying.'

'Not for kissing me?' He spiked his fingers into her hair, pressing her cheek into his chest. 'Well, if you're not sorry, perhaps we can...'

She gulped in another breath, but her shoulders stopped heaving. She shook her head.

'No, Will. Stop it.' She lifted her head and looked up at him. His eyes were serious, his mouth, which had almost driven her over the edge, was a straight, composed line.

Scarlett shifted until she could lean her back against his chest. He wrapped his arms across her waist and his thighs pressed lightly against hers. She felt safe and protected. She rested the back of her head on his shoulder and felt the brush of his jaw across her temple. She knew that she wanted to tell him.

'We were engaged.'

Will lifted her left hand and ran his thumb over the faint mark on her finger.

'I know.'

'He recruited me to join his research team, so I was already flattered. Then when he paid me attention that was more than professional, I was more flattered still.' She wriggled to get more comfortable. 'I was so, so naïve.'

'Don't beat yourself up, Scarlett. It wasn't your fault.'

'If I hadn't been so desperate to find some sort of security—*stability*—I might have been more clear-sighted. *Strong-willed*.' She huffed out a sigh. 'Marguerite's house had been sold to pay for her care, and I was losing her too, a little more each time I visited. I clung to the first straw that floated past and unfortunately it was Alan. I know now that he'd identified me as someone who could be useful to him in the research field. I'd built up a bit of a reputation…'

'For being good at what you did?'

She nodded. 'He was putting together a team for the Amazon expedition, looking for the orchid I told you about, and he took me with him. I didn't want to go—there were others who deserved the trip more—but he insisted. Then he proposed. Now I think he did it so I wouldn't back out.'

'What made you end it?'

Scarlett chewed her lip, struggling to frame the sentence she'd never spoken out loud.

'He abandoned me in the jungle.'

'So the reports on the internet were true.'

His arms tightened around her, but his chin lifted from the crown of her head. 'Tell me what happened.'

'He left me behind. The team had divided into two and he and I had been trekking for three days. It was tough. Hot, obviously, but so much more than that. He was bad-tempered and critical. Everything either stung or bit. Although, if you could ignore all that, it was very beautiful and so full of energy, teeming with life.'

She could feel his heartbeat against her back and the rise and fall of his breathing, but Will had assumed an absolute stillness.

'Go on.' She felt the words rumble in his chest.

'I found the orchid. I thought he'd be pleased but he seemed angry. He took photos of it, and we mapped its position and then he said we should head back towards the main camp. "Mission Impossible accomplished". Those were his words.'

'Sounds like a pompous bastard.'

She felt his anger in the way his arms tightened around her.

'The rainforest is dense, and so full of noise, it's possible to get disorientated very quickly. I moved on a bit, looking for more flowers, thinking he'd wait for me, and then I couldn't find him, or the orchid. I think he dug it up. He didn't get the memo about taking nothing away and leaving... nothing behind.'

Her body tensed, remembered panic tugging at her. Will lifted a hand and grazed his knuckles across her cheek.

'It's okay.' His voice was rough. 'I've got you. You're safe.'

She swallowed.

'The jungle covers tracks very, very quickly, and the canopy is dense. It's hard to fix on a direction without reference points or the sun. I was lost within minutes.'

'For how long?'

'Six nights.

'I had some biscuits in my backpack and there's an endless supply of water. Because of my botanical knowledge I knew I could eat some of the fruit and plants.'

Will swore.

'I did panic, in the first few hours, but I managed to do one sensible thing, which was to follow a stream flowing downhill. I came to a small settlement where the people were kind and took me to a larger one. From there someone took me upriver, back to the camp. The others weren't surprised to see me. Alan had returned to England, saying I'd chosen to stay in the jungle with some local people for a few days.'

'He'd gone back to England? Presumably to claim the discovery of the plant as his own?'

She shrugged. 'That's what he did. But if he stole it, he can't let anyone else see it. If he did, his reputation in the scientific community would be destroyed.'

'But you haven't let him get away with it? You've reported him?'

'It's his word against mine, and it happened a long way from English law. He knew I had no family, and it would be a while before my friends began to wonder where I was. And if the question arose, I *had* been with local people. That suited him perfectly. Communication is difficult and sketchy in those conditions. Things get lost in translation. I was never going to be able to prove what he'd done.'

'He hoped he'd never see you again.'

'His wish has been granted. He need never see me again now. But he knows what he did.'

'It sounds as though that won't bother him for a moment. I'd like to…'

'Please don't tell me what you'd like to do to him. I might have nightmares.'

She felt spent, a lethargy creeping over her which she knew came partly from the relief of telling the story. She didn't want to accept that the other part came from the security she found, wrapped in Will's arms, feeling the regular thump of his heart beating with hers. This was a false security. It could never last.

'*Do* you have nightmares?'

'Sometimes I have to sleep with the light on. But now I only have myself to believe in, and I'm determined that I will. I thought he loved me. How could I have got it so wrong?'

Will dropped his cheek onto her hair. When he eventually spoke, his voice was muffled.

'Do you still love him?'

She knew the answer she should give. It was the only logical one, and she felt in the hitch of his breath, as she hesitated, that it was the one he wanted to hear.

'I...don't know if I ever really did. I hate him for what he did. I despise him. Love shouldn't be something you can simply switch off. It has to fade until it turns into something weak that no longer has the power to control or hurt. I thought I loved him, but now I can't even remember how that felt. I think for me he was a convenient safety net and he manipulated me into believing him. I think my judgement is flawed—skewed by my childhood experience of love, or the lack of it. If I can't trust myself, how can I ever learn to trust someone else? And I believe trust has to be a fundamental part of love.'

Will abandoned his desk. He'd given up trying to concentrate on anything constructive, his thoughts filled with the man who had been happy to leave Scarlett in the jungle, perhaps hoping she'd never find her way out. Prepared to destroy her life, her ability to love, her willingness to trust, for the sake of being a footnote in the world of botany.

He found her acceptance of such a shattering betrayal incredible. He'd have wanted to go after the man—Alan—and throw every book at him, legal or otherwise. He'd have wanted to see him brought down.

But, he wondered, how would that have been for Scarlett? It would have dragged her name into the public eye, a sordid case of betrayal for the media to pick over and then discard. Better that she'd left Alan with his small triumph and the corrosive knowledge of what he'd done.

Rozendal had come to her when she'd needed it most. But the visit to the pool high in the mountains had not only been to show it to Scarlett. After his discussions with the engineering company in Cape Town which specialised in hydraulic machinery, he knew the pool and waterfall would serve his purpose perfectly.

If he explained his intentions to Scarlett, would she see his point of view? Harnessing the river would go against all her principles of rewilding and returning the land to its natural state. But the future of Bellevale might stand or fall on the supply of water from Rozendal. The river had never been known to dry up, even in times of drought.

But if he acted on his feelings for her, would he simply be manipulating her into giving him what he wanted? He couldn't do that to her, or to himself.

It was late and very dark when he left the house. The scorching wind had turned chilly, carrying with it the scent of rain.

His nightly walk took him around the edge of the vineyards, past the cellars, the restaurant and the cottages. He narrowed his eyes, looking through the trees towards Vineyard Cottage. A glimmer of light flickered through the restless branches. Was Scarlett sleeping with the light on tonight?

A single thought beat in his brain: was she all right?

The security light came on as he leapt up the steps and knocked on the door.

'Scarlett?'

It could only have been thirty seconds before the door opened, but it felt like for ever.

'Will? What…?'

'It's late and your light was on.'

She stepped back. 'Come in.'

'Are you okay?' His eyes took in her cotton shorts and camisole, pink gingham with a satin bow. His mouth dried. This was a bad idea. Of course she was all right. She'd think he was crazy. And he was, he admitted silently. Crazy for her.

'Not really.'

She'd caught the sun and her cheeks and nose were tinged with pink but beneath that her skin was white. She looked exhausted.

'You look tired. You should be in bed.'

'I might have to remind you that you're bossy, and telling a woman she looks tired is not normally regarded as a compliment.'

'Yeah, you might, but it won't make a damn bit of difference. You look as if you need a good night's sleep.'

Scarlett lifted her arms and bunched her hair in her hands. He tried to keep his eyes from straying down to the narrow band of skin which appeared as the camisole rode upwards.

'I tried sleep. It didn't work out.'

'Any reason why?'

'You noticed the light was on so you know why, Will.' Without warning, she put her hands to her face. 'Will…'

In two strides he had his arms around her. She didn't resist him, falling against him, her arms banding across his back.

'It's okay. I've got you.' He smoothed a hand through the silky length of her hair, resting his cheek on her head, breathing in her scent of flowers and rain.

'It's not okay. I'm afraid to fall asleep. Talking has brought it all back, in HD and Surround Sound. I have my own private IMAX theatre in my head. Every sound I hear takes me back there.'

Her voice rose. 'If I put out the light, I hear the jungle closing in on me. I should never have told you about it. I should have kept it locked up, where I didn't have to admit it was true.'

'Scarlett.' He felt the almost imperceptible release of tension in her body. 'I'm so sorry, but I'm glad I saw your light was on.'

'I wanted to call you.'

'Why didn't you?'

'Because I have to manage this on my own.'

'No, you don't. I want to kill him for what he did to you.'

'Thank you, but I don't think that would help.'

'What *would* help?'

She was quiet, then she took a deep breath and spoke. 'You help. You've made me see I can still have fun.'

His fingers followed the line of her spine up her back, exploring. He discovered that her breath stuttered when he found a particular place under her left shoulder blade. His other hand rested on her hip, his thumb tracing a circle over the bone beneath the cotton of her shorts. Her breath had become quick and shallow, feathering over his skin at the vee of his sweater.

The wildness of their earlier kiss had to be contained. He didn't want to frighten her by losing control. And, he told himself, he didn't want to scare himself either.

'Will?'

'Mmm? Tell me how I can help…'

'Kiss me.'

'Scarlett…'

'Please. It'll help…'

She moved a hand from his back and lifted his palm from her hip, drawing it up close to his chest. Her thumb moved over the inside of his wrist.

He felt his restraint dissolving, his willpower falling away, and all that was left was the need to kiss her, absorb her scent, close any gaps that remained between them.

'God, Scarlett,' he breathed. 'Are you sure?'

'Yes.' The word was scarcely more than an exhale. 'When we kiss I forget everything else.'

When their lips met, tentatively, he buried his hands in her hair, holding her head steady. Her eyes were dark with desire, a deep sea-green. Her lips, pink and so soft, parted as his mouth hovered over hers, inviting him in.

It was deep, immediately, as if the previous times had been preliminaries which they could skip now. His tongue probed the astonishing sweetness of her mouth, intimate and explicit. Soft sounds of pleasure and need came from her throat, making him band her to his hard body more tightly.

It wasn't enough. This would never be enough. He slid a hand down her back, slipping his fingers into the waistband of her shorts, and she arched into him.

All thought vanished from his brain except the

knowledge that this was what he wanted and the joy that she wanted it too. Her warm skin and silky hair drove him wild. He wanted to bury his face in the russet mass and lose himself in her completely.

Holding her steady, he kissed her still, while one hand roamed her body, eliciting gasps of response and shivers of ecstasy. She felt like molten fire in his arms, hot and dangerous but irresistible.

His hand came to rest on her ribcage and then his palm brushed over her straining breast.

At last, he stopped the kiss. He needed to feel her skin against his, see her perfect body, wanting him. He lifted her arms, gripped the edge of the camisole and pulled it over her head, dropping it on the floor.

For a moment he drank in the sight of her. Her ivory skin glowing in the soft light, the curve of her waist and dip of her navel. Her perfect breasts, rosy tipped. Her lips, red and swollen from his mouth and her eyes, hazy with desire.

'You're the most beautiful thing I've ever seen. Scarlett...'

Then he put an arm behind her knees and lifted her against him. She pulled his head down towards her, fusing her mouth with his, as he carried her to the bedroom.

CHAPTER EIGHTEEN

SCARLET LIFTED HEAVY LIDS. Grey light filtered through the shutters and she heard the muted thrum of rain on the thatch.

It had been raining for three days and nights, ever since she and Will...

She turned her head on the pillow, not surprised to see the space next to her was empty. He left her as dawn broke. He liked to start work early, he said, before the endless interruptions began. She could still feel the weight of his arm across her body.

But he hadn't left, she realised, as she heard a tap running in the bathroom, the clink as he hung up a towel on the metal ring.

A minute later he crossed the dim room and sat on the edge of the bed next to her.

'Hey.'

He bent and kissed her, slowly and thoroughly. She slipped a hand round the back of his neck, her fingers into his hair, raking her nails lightly across his scalp.

He groaned and moved her hand away. 'Enough. I need to go. But I'll see you later. I've booked a table for us in the restaurant tonight.'

Her eyes widened. 'Are you sure? Are we celebrating something?'

'No.' He ran a finger down her cheek, his thumb across her bottom lip. 'But there's something I'd like to talk about.'

'We can make it a celebration of my move.'

'Your move? You're going somewhere?'

'The two weeks are up, Will. I'm moving into Rozendal today.'

'But the thatching isn't finished yet. The rain…' He glanced towards the window. 'Listen to it.'

'It's a beautiful sound, and the house is water-proof under that tarpaulin. Not a drop of rain has found its way in. I've painted my bedroom, the bed has arrived, with my gorgeous new linen, the bath-room and kitchen work, mostly. It's all worked out.'

His jaw tightened and she put a hand against his cheek.

'Stay a bit longer.'

'Two weeks was the deal, Will. I don't want any more favours, remember. Anyway, Vineyard Cottage is probably booked from today.'

He shook his head. 'I booked it for a month, in my name. You can stay.'

Scarlett shuffled up the bed and leaned against the headboard. She tucked the duvet around her as his eyes darkened, fixing on the shadowed dip between her breasts. Desire tightened her abdomen.

'Being able to stay here has been a lifesaver for me, Will, but I want to move. And it is a cause for celebration. It's the first home of my own I've ever had.'

'Yes, I know.' He pulled a hand over the back of his head. 'It's just that...'

'This is convenient for us, I know.' Each night he'd come to her after his late walk, when the rest of the estate was asleep, and he left early. She didn't think anyone else knew they were sleeping together.

To be with her at Rozendal he'd have to drive over, and back. Perhaps he'd no longer want to spend the night in her bed.

She'd told herself that was fine, but now, faced with the reality of it, she felt less certain. The thought of him not being there, warm and responsive, when she woke in the night, made her feel hollow. She loved waking and turning into his arms, finding his mouth, feeling his body respond to her. She loved the way he tucked her against him, his chin resting on her head, as they drifted off to sleep.

How would she cope if it ended? She couldn't begin to imagine. They were so perfect together. Without him, she was afraid she'd never feel complete again.

How had she allowed this to happen?

'Convenient, yes.' He nodded.

'Not romantic.'

'I don't do romantic, Scarlett.'

'I know.'

'That's okay, then.' He smiled, his dimple creasing his freshly shaven cheek. He reached out to run a finger along her skin above the duvet, pausing at the dip in her cleavage. 'Go back to sleep,

Scarlett. It's early.' He kissed her forehead. 'I'll collect you at seven-thirty for dinner.'

'From Rozendal.'

Scarlett had spent the day moving into her home.

The house still looked like a building site, but it was dry, and she thought her bedroom was beautiful. She'd painted it a shade of soft white and had a cream carpet laid. Her new bed, dressed in a cream silk valance, had a curved headboard covered in buttoned, pale grey velvet. She'd made it up with the fine cotton sheets and duvet she'd chosen, edged with delicate embroidery. A luxurious velvet throw lay folded across the foot.

Nightstands, lamps and a dressing table were on order, but she was happy to wait for them. Nothing could blunt the excitement of spending her first night at Rozendal.

She'd showered in the ancient bathroom. The water was hot and clean, although the pressure wavered between force eight and a trickle.

On a visit to Franschhoek, choosing paint colours for the drawing room, she'd fallen in love with a green watered silk dress, and now she was glad she'd bought it. Since she would be dining with the owner, she supposed she could wear whatever she liked to The Stable Yard Restaurant, but the occasion felt special enough for her to dress up.

She was waiting on the veranda when the Range

Rover pulled up. She watched Will climb the steps towards her and her heart turned over in her chest.

It was hard to believe that this man had shared her bed for the past three nights. She knew the long, sleek planes of his body almost as well as her own. She knew how his shoulders felt beneath her hands, how he liked the feeling of her fingers raking across his back and chest. She could make him gasp with pleasure by kissing him along the collarbone, or groan with need by trailing her fingers across the small of his back.

Their lovemaking was gentle and slow or quick and sometimes a little rough, but he was considerate, always asking if she was all right, calming her with tender kisses when she called his name, and holding her as she fell asleep.

The nightmares had faded; the memories of Alan had shrunk into insignificance. Nothing that had gone before could compare with how she felt in Will's arms.

He reached the top step and wrapped her in a hug, kissing her hair and tipping her face up to move his lips to her mouth.

'Scarlett. You look…breathtaking,' he murmured, between kisses. 'Did you buy that dress to match your eyes, or was that an accident?'

She laughed. 'Did you wear that shirt to match yours?' She slid two fingers between the buttons and scraped his skin, feeling goosebumps roughen the smoothness. 'Oh, your eyes are darker now. Not such a good match.'

'Any more of that and I won't need a shirt at all, because we won't be going to dinner. We'll be going to bed.'

'Mmm. But I'm hungry.'

'So am I, but there're different sorts of hunger.'

'Perhaps we can satisfy them all?' She withdrew her fingers.

'If we're going to have time for that we'd better get started.'

Grace met them at the entrance to the restaurant.

'I've put you at your usual table, Will.'

She led them past the bar, busy with guests enjoying pre-dinner drinks, to a table in a corner next to a tall window, with a view of the room and of the garden. The vineyards beyond had already faded into the evening light, and the spectacular mountain backdrop was dark against the azure sky.

Scarlett knew the restaurant was famous for its relaxed atmosphere and superb food. The kitchen was visible at one end over a modern granite worktop, but the rest of the interior had a timeless charm, with a terracotta tiled floor, white walls and reminders of the building's original purpose.

'I'm surprised you don't prefer one of those tables.' She looked towards the back wall, where several of the stalls had been converted into private, intimate dining spaces.

Will shook his head, holding her chair for her. 'I like to see who else is here. And this table is quite secluded.'

He closed the menu and handed it back to their server. 'I'll order for both of us.'

'Bossy?'

'No. It's all good.' His eyes met hers, navy blue and filled with intent. 'And...' his voice dropped, warm and smoky '...I know what you like.'

'I might prefer the tasting menu.'

'You can have that later.'

Scarlett had to admit that he was right. The food was delicious, and he'd chosen the perfect pairing of wines.

Will lifted a bottle from the bucket at his elbow and topped up her glass. He raised his own, his eyes intent on her face.

'Here's to my new home,' she said, touching her glass to his. 'Is that what you want to talk about?'

He replaced his glass but kept his fingers on the stem. Scarlett swallowed as she watched them caress the delicate crystal, then she pulled her eyes away, trying to compose her expression.

'In a way, yes.'

Something in his eyes released a curl of unease in her. His gaze was intent on her, but it was because he was watching for her reaction to whatever he was going to say, not because he was remembering how it felt to kiss her or hold her. Some part of him had withdrawn.

She folded her hands in her lap and straightened her spine, leaning away from him.

'What is it, Will? And why do I think I'm not going to like it?'

He lifted his chin, a shadow of surprise flickering in his eyes.

'I'd like,' he said, 'to buy a part of Rozendal.'

The disquiet faded a little. This wasn't news. She'd known it since she'd stepped into the middle of that auction. Was he going to make her an offer he thought she wouldn't refuse? Did he even *know* the size of the fortune Marguerite had left her? Had he not even begun to understand the reasons why she'd never give up Rozendal?

Then the disquiet returned. Did he think sleeping with her for three nights would have made her easier to persuade? She crushed that thought. He was private, difficult to get to know, and complicated, but she didn't think he was manipulative, and she didn't think he could have faked what they'd shared...but then she remembered how she'd asked him to kiss her—made it plain that she wanted him to take her to bed.

I haven't had fun for a long time... she'd said.

For him, had it just been fun?

It had become so much more than fun, for her.

Smoothing the white linen napkin over her knees, she met his steady gaze with her own.

'Only a part of it? I thought you wanted all of

it, and me out of the way.' She tried to smile. 'And I thought you never changed your mind?'

Will felt cornered. That was what happened when you set such categorical boundaries for yourself, he thought, but it was the only way he knew how to live his life. He'd declared he would own Rozendal, but he now had to admit that in Scarlett he'd met his match. She was not going to take the money and run.

She had every reason to stay at Rozendal indefinitely and to put her New Age ideas into practice, when he could be using the land to increase the size of his estate, turn the house into a high-end boutique hotel and restore the boundaries to their original configuration, before one of his feckless ancestors had sold out to one of the du Valois family.

Moreover, the past three nights had seen him break his own unwritten rule, for the first time ever. He'd spent three nights in her bed, and if his brain had told him he was being reckless, compromising his safety for the sake of waking up and finding her in his arms, his body would have told his rational mind to go to hell, because every second had been exquisite, every touch mind-blowing.

She was not in the market for permanence and that suited him just fine. After her experience with her previous partner—her *fiancé*—she'd admitted she'd never trust anyone again; in future she'd only ever depend on herself.

Faced with her absolute determination to carry out her plans, he'd changed tack. *His* plans for Rozendal could be shelved, for a while at least, but he needed the rights to the pool and river.

He had all the facts and figures at his fingertips, and he expressed them fluently and clearly. But he could see stubborn refusal gaining strength in her eyes. What was that she'd said about being strong-minded? Here was the proof.

She listened, but she interrupted him.

'I plan to use the water from the river, and to encourage the natural development of the riverbank, once the invasive plants have been eradicated, Will.' She began to shred a bread roll onto her side plate. 'Your plan doesn't allow for that.'

He had an answer. 'If your estate is truly to be returned to its natural state, you shouldn't use the river for irrigating or watering. You should rely on the seasonal rainfall.'

'The rose garden was famous once, and I intend to make it famous again. I'm not rewilding that; I'm restoring it, like the house. I need the water for the garden. The river has never dried up, ever, and that means I can rely on it.'

'How do you know it's never dried up?'

'One of the elderly men helping me in the garden told me. It's well known amongst the local community that there is always water at Rozendal, even in the most severe drought. I don't intend to change that. The river is not for sale.'

Will felt frustration rising, tightening in a band

around his chest, making his jaw ache. He gripped his hands together on the tabletop, hanging onto his temper.

'I don't understand,' he said at last, 'why you want to turn the clock back, impose the past on the present and the future. It's counter-productive…'

'Will.' Her voice was quiet, but he recognised the thread of steel running through it which he'd only heard when she was expressing her passion for the land. 'I'm rescuing species that have thrived here for millennia, but which will disappear in a generation if they're not given the space and conditions they need to grow.' She drew a deep breath. 'Rewilding restores relationships between animals, plants and the environment. I'm not turning my back on science or imposing the past. I'm applying a different science and securing the future.'

'Scarlett.' Her eyes softened a fraction but her body still looked taut as a bowstring. 'You and I…'

He thought he saw a faint tremor in her bottom lip, but her teeth closed over it briefly and her mouth firmed.

'When you asked me to come here for dinner, Will, I thought perhaps it was you and me you wanted to talk about.' He tried to interrupt her, but she raised a hand. 'No. Let me finish. Please.' She dropped her hand to the tablecloth and his eyes went to the almost invisible evidence of her past trauma. Hot, acid guilt made him look away. 'I thought you might want to discuss how we might…manage…once I'd moved into Rozendal. I'm aware you want to keep our…*us*…a secret. That's fine. It'll be less messy when we decide to end it, if nobody else is aware of it.'

'*End* it? Scarlett, it's not…'

'I don't know what it is, Will. I don't know what's between us. Perhaps we're just two people who need each other at this moment, for different reasons. Neither of us wants a permanent relationship.' She hoped he didn't notice the tremor in her voice. 'But I hope… *I hope*…you haven't thought having sex with me would make me easier to persuade. I enjoy your company. The sex is off the scale, but if it's had any other purpose for you besides enjoying it, your behaviour is little better than Alan's.'

Will pushed a hand through his hair, adrenalin burning through him, trying to find the words to convince her that she was wrong, but his brain had gone into a tailspin and if he didn't find a way to pull it back soon, like in the next few seconds, he was going to crash and burn.

'That's not true,' he grated at last. 'He left you in the jungle. You might have died and never been found.' He tried to take her hand, but she moved it away. 'I would never, ever do anything to hurt you. Being with you is like nothing I've ever experienced before, and I don't only mean being in bed with you.' He wiped a hand over his face, searching for the right words. 'You make me smile. You challenge me. You make me want to…'

'What, Will?'

'You make me want to break all the rules, but I daren't…'

He raised his head, scanning the busy restaurant, hoping nobody would notice the drama playing out in the corner. Grace caught his eye across the room. She looked anxious and she shook her head, her gaze sliding away from his, to a noisy crowd around the bar.

She set off towards them, weaving quickly between the tables before arriving at theirs.

'I'm sorry, Will. They came in with a group. Their names weren't on the list…'

'Who?' He was aware of Scarlett turning her head to look at him, but he followed Grace's gaze.

His body stilled; every muscle tensed.

'Will? Are you okay? You've gone very white.' Scarlett's voice seemed to come from far away, but he knew she was right there, where he wished he knew she'd stay. But that was unrealistic. Women didn't stay. They grabbed the next, better opportunity and left ruins in their wake.

He'd let her get too close. Dropped his guard and let her in.

'Will?'

He turned to look at her, to tell her they had to leave, and saw her expression change, her look of concern replaced by one of incredulity, and he understood it perfectly. Because coming towards them, his eyes fixed on Scarlett, was his identical twin brother, and behind him was the wife who should have been his.

CHAPTER NINETEEN

UTTER CONFUSION SWAMPED SCARLETT. She felt like an audience of one, watching a play unfold and she didn't understand the plot or even the language.

She saw the moment Will used his iron will to crush his emotions. He stood, every movement spare and controlled, and watched his brother approach.

She rose to stand beside him.

'Will!'

Up close, subtle differences emerged between the two men. Richard was fractionally shorter than Will, and of a lighter, softer physique. There was no evidence of the hard, toned muscle which she knew lay beneath Will's linen shirt. Richard's dark hair was longer, slightly unkempt. But it was his eyes that marked him out as different from his brother. There was no warmth in his ice-blue appraisal.

'Richard.' Will extended his hand for the briefest of greetings. His eyes flicked to the small, curvy woman at Richard's side. 'Melanie.'

'Good to see you, bro. And with a stunning companion…?'

'This is Scarlett.'

Scarlett nodded to them both.

Melanie laughed. 'Scarlett? Well-named.'

'Scarlett and I were just leaving.'

As he moved around the table she entwined her fingers with his.

He turned to look at her. His eyes rested on her face, faintly surprised, and she squeezed his hand tightly. The surprise faded, to be replaced with something that shook her to the core. He held her gaze for seconds and then he turned away, but Scarlett had recognised what she'd seen in his eyes because the connection which had arced between them in that moment was as strong as titanium but gentle as dew.

'Oh…' Richard stepped back. 'I was hoping we could have a chat, Will. Scarlett and Melanie could get to know each other…'

'We have nothing to say to one another, Richard, and Scarlett and Melanie don't need to get to know each other. I doubt they would have anything in common.'

Scarlett felt him urging her close to his side. He untangled his fingers from hers and clamped his arm around her waist, walking her towards the door.

It had all taken less than two minutes. Was that enough time for her whole world to have changed?

Grim-faced, his knuckles white on the steering wheel, Will brought the Range Rover to a jerky stop in front of Rozendal. The rain had begun to fall again, sifting down in drenching sheets.

'Would you like to come in?'

Will shook his head.

She jumped from the car and raced up the steps, out of the rain. He hadn't uttered a word since leaving the restaurant and she didn't expect him to follow her. He needed time to gather himself, she thought. He needed space.

She didn't understand the extreme animosity between him and his brother. She longed to hold him, to try to soothe him, but she would hold back—let him come to her when he was ready.

'Scarlett.' The strain in his voice tore at her heart. She turned, ready to take him in her arms.

His expression stopped her in her tracks, stealing her breath. Her heart began to hammer at her ribs.

'Will? What's wrong?'

He shook his head, then pushed his damp hair off his forehead. 'I'm sorry.'

'Sorry? It wasn't your fault. You didn't know...'

'No, I'm sorry for this. For us.'

Her disquiet swelled into something much more dangerous. Fear lapped at her, like a malevolent tide. She'd vowed no man—no other person— would ever again wield power over her emotions. What didn't kill you made you stronger, and she was alive. She was the independent woman Marguerite had exhorted her to be. Wasn't she?

But what she'd seen in Will's eyes had destroyed all that. It had been the briefest flash, but she'd seen it and she'd known she was lost.

'What about us?' Her voice came out as a whisper.

'I haven't been honest with you, Scarlett.' He

pushed his hands into his pockets and moved back a step. 'I might have let you think there was something between us, and I'm sorry if I've misled you.'

'*Misled* me? How?'

'I thought I might be able to convince you to sell to me—first the whole estate, but then the pool and water rights.' He shrugged, the movement of his wide shoulders brief, and she wondered how he could be so cool, when her heart was being ripped to shreds.

'That's all you wanted?' Her hands hurt as she twisted them together.

His eyes were devoid of emotion, his mouth set. That mouth…

'Yes.'

Her head snapped back, as if he'd hit her. She wouldn't think about his mouth ever again. Or his hands, or…

Her silk dress was spattered with raindrops, and she shivered with cold. She bit her bottom lip, hard, the hurt helping her to focus on something other than his crushing words. She stared at him.

'You said I'd be lying if I denied there was anything between us, Will, and I don't know why you're denying it now. You weren't quick enough to hide your true feelings. I saw, and I don't believe you. It's you who's being untruthful, to me and to yourself.'

Will drained his glass. He'd lost count of how many shots of whisky he'd drunk, and he didn't care.

His head throbbed with fatigue, but the alcohol had neither numbed his pain, stilled his fear or knocked him out.

It would be a waste of a good hangover.

He was waiting for the light to begin to silver the dark sky behind the mountains. Then he'd take a shower, cold if he could bear it, drink black coffee, as hot as possible, and, as soon as the time was civilised, he'd go to Rozendal.

He'd tried to blank her agonised expression from his mind, without success. He'd chosen each word to crush her, and he thought he'd succeeded. But then she'd accused him of lying.

How could she see into his soul with such clarity when his own perception of things was so muddled? He cursed Richard and Melanie for showing up at the one restaurant in the Cape where they were explicitly unwelcome. But he despised himself for not handling the encounter with more dignity. He should be able to dismiss them with the lack of regard and attention they deserved.

He hated the thought that Scarlett had seen his reaction, and he intended to attempt to explain it to her. If she was going to judge him, she needed, at least, to have all the facts.

At eight-thirty he pulled up outside Rozendal, parking amidst the builders' trucks and decorators' vans. Rain dripped at a steady rate off the giant tarpaulin covering the house and the steps looked slippery. He should warn Scarlett…

Scarlett, he thought, would dismiss his warning with contempt.

She stood outside the broad front door. The brass handles she'd polished with such enthusiasm shone. She wore jeans and a jacket and her hair was in a neat French braid. A set of car keys jingled in one hand, and she held the handle of her small cabin bag in the other.

Shock punched him in the gut. He tried to breathe in, but oxygen seemed to be in short supply.

'What are you doing here, Will?'

'Why? I… You're going away. Where to?'

'I don't know why it concerns you. I'm sure you'll be pleased not to have me around.' She took a step forward. 'I'm going to England.'

'*England?* Why?'

'For some reason I was having trouble sleeping and I checked my emails early this morning. My father is ill.'

'You're going to see your parents? But I thought you had no contact with them…'

'I've always made sure they could contact me if necessary, and now they have.'

'That's outrageous. All these years…everything you've been through, and they've never supported you. Yet you get one email and you're going…'

'They're my parents, Will, and they have nobody else. I'm going to see if I can help them. I'm grateful that I can.'

Will propped himself against the balustrade. 'I think you're crazy.'

'What you think doesn't matter. I'm doing what's right for me. Possibly you should try reaching out to your family, instead of perpetuating an argument you've already won.'

Anger, hot and damaging, coursed through his veins. He folded his arms to stop himself from punching the wall.

'Scarlett, you have no idea what you're talking about.'

'Well, try explaining it to me then, Will.' She glanced at her watch. 'You have approximately five minutes.'

Will swallowed, at a loss as to how to do this. The words to articulate exactly what had happened were buried deep inside him. They'd never been used. He had to dig deep. Breathing was suddenly painful, his constricted lungs unwilling to expand.

'She was going to marry me. Melanie. We were engaged.'

The words hung between them, out in the universe for ever. Watching the colour drain from Scarlett's face should have given him a scrap of satisfaction but it made the hurt worse.

'Oh, Will. I'm… That's shocking. I'm so sorry.'

'Don't be,' he snapped. 'I'm grateful not to be married to someone who could do what she did.'

'Yes…yes, I think you should be.' She stepped forward, putting out a hand towards him, but he flinched away, out of her reach. 'What happened?'

'I…' He rubbed his burning eyes, raw from lack of sleep, wishing he could leave now, and not go through with saying this. 'I'd taken ownership of Bellevale. It took two years to get into shape, to be able to start planning to expand, open the restaurant, convert the cottages. Melanie is an events organiser, and she came to look at it with a view to using it as a wedding venue.'

'You don't do weddings.'

'We don't. She fell in love with the idea of the place—its romantic past, the old buildings, even older oaks. She decided the first showcase wedding, which would attract dozens of other would-be couples to tie the knot, would be ours. I was sucked into it. I was working eighteen-hour days, seven days a week, to get the vineyards productive, to become successful. Success has always been my goal. I've always had to win.' He shook his head. 'Sometimes I wish I was less competitive. I didn't notice that Melanie was growing dissatisfied. She'd met Richard in Cape Town and decided life with him would be a lot more fun than with me. He had the money and didn't have to work. I was determined to make Bellevale a huge success and never stopped long enough to see it wasn't the life she'd envisaged, as my wife.'

Scarlett nodded. Her teeth were fastened, hard, on her bottom lip. He wanted to reach out and run his thumb over her mouth, tell her to stop it, but he could no longer claim that privilege.

'She and Richard married at what should have been her wedding to me. She said she refused to let all that organisation go to waste. It was the first and last wedding to be held at Bellevale.'

'Will, I'm sorry. I should have realised there was a good reason behind your estrangement from your family. Your parents…?'

'Couldn't see what the fuss was about. From the time Richard was born, seventeen minutes before me, he'd always come first. That's why I always have to win. Coming second at anything is never good enough. I hope seeing your parents brings you some closure. Just don't judge me for not seeing mine.'

He fixed his eyes on her face, trying to imprint all its details on his memory. Her beautiful amber hair; her eyes that changed from emerald in the sunshine to deepest forest in his arms at night; her full bottom lip which felt like peach blossom under his thumb and tasted like honey on his tongue; the ivory skin of her throat, where that pulse reacted so swiftly to his touch.

Then he stepped back.

'Will?'

'Yes?'

'Do you still love her?' Her voice was unsteady.

He knew the words which would keep him safe. If he said them, he'd drive her away for ever, and that was what he needed to do. But she'd already accused him once of lying and he knew he had to be honest.

'No,' he said. 'I realised last night that I never had.'

CHAPTER TWENTY

SCARLETT LEANED AGAINST the sink. Grey rain lashed the windows and cold seeped up through the tiles under her feet. The mountain had almost disappeared under a thick layer of cloud.

She pressed the heels of her hands into her eye sockets, trying to relieve the ache of fatigue. Getting her parents settled into their assisted living apartment and putting their cottage on the market had been stressful. The journey to London from Yorkshire had been long, and even though the overnight flight had felt interminable she had dreaded arriving.

But now that she was here she needed to contact Will as quickly as possible. She wanted to control the situation, not dread bumping into him by chance. She did not want to see him at all, but she had to tell him how she felt, whatever the outcome. She pulled her phone from her bag and scrolled through it, then she took a deep breath and unblocked his number. She'd bring in her luggage and then she'd call him.

Her phone beeped as she stepped back through the door. His name on the screen confused her. How did he know she was back? She'd told nobody she was coming home. She read the message and her hands began to shake. He'd tried repeatedly to contact her, he said. He was trying this last time before leaving for the airport, on his way to find her in England.

Scarlett looked at the time and picked up the car keys, her heart racing. She'd be too late to stop him if he really was leaving immediately. But she might be able to catch up with him at the airport. Her fatigue forgotten, she ran out onto the veranda and down the slippery steps.

The road to Bellevale was awash. It looked as if the rain hadn't stopped since she'd left, a month ago. She groaned in frustration as she had to slow down to negotiate a flood where the river went under the bridge. Then she accelerated, not caring if she hit a hidden pothole or skidded around a corner. She swung the car between the white gateposts and continued up the drive between the avenue of oaks.

The Range Rover stood in front of the homestead and she exhaled. Then she thought he might have taken a taxi, or Grace might have driven him. The car slewed to a stop on the sodden gravel and she flung herself out of it, up the steps and through the front door.

'Scarlett?' He looked more shocked than she felt. 'What are you doing here?'

'I…got your message.'

'I'm…' He pulled a hand over his face in the gesture she had grown to love in a few short weeks. 'When did you arrive?'

'This morning.' She moved further into the hall. A suitcase stood at the door, a jacket on top of it.

'I've been trying to contact you…'

'If you'd like me to go…'

'You didn't answer your phone or pick up messages.'

'I blocked your number.'

'Grace wouldn't tell me how to find you. Nor would your lawyers. I practically begged.'

'I'm glad to hear they listened to me. Only I didn't ask Grace…'

'She said I should leave you alone and you'd contact me if you wanted to.'

'Good advice. What did you want to say to me?'

'That you were right.'

'I thought that was your prerogative. Aren't you always right?'

'Scarlett, please…just listen to me?'

She felt as though she was held together by a single thread which was in imminent danger of snapping and allowing her to unravel in an untidy and messy heap at Will's feet.

'Okay. I'm sorry. I'm tired and…' She wanted to add that she was sad. That the past month had been the hardest of her life. That her heart had lurched every time she remembered a snatch of conversation they'd had or glimpsed a bottle of Bellevale wine on a supermarket shelf. Who knew there were so many ways in which she could remember him, and every one hurt.

'You were right. I lied, because I was afraid. I thought I was immune, after what happened with Melanie and Richard. I thought no one could ever get past my guard. I was determined never to let anyone close to me, so that I could never be hurt or humiliated again. I'd fought against being second-best all my life, and I'd finally achieved what I wanted. Then Melanie and Richard...'

'It was a double betrayal, Will. I don't know how you deal with something like that.'

'You were betrayed in a much worse way, yet you didn't want revenge. And you owed your parents nothing, yet when they needed you...' He took a step towards her. 'You enchanted me, Scarlett. I wanted to be with you and then I realised I was in too deep. It terrified me. I'd broken all my own rules and I was spinning out of control. I deliberately set out to hurt you, to drive you away, because that was the only way I could see of protecting myself. It was cowardly and unforgivable and if you never want to see me again I'll understand, but I need you to know how sorry I am.'

'Will, I knew you were lying because of what I saw in your eyes that night. My whole world turned upside down because I knew I'd broken my own rules too, by falling in love with you. I never wanted to depend on anyone else ever again, but I knew at that moment that we were soulmates and without you I'd always feel incomplete. When you told me you only wanted the water rights, my heart broke. I knew it wasn't true and that you were afraid of what had happened between us, but you wouldn't let me help you.'

Somehow, his arms were around her in an embrace so tight she could scarcely breathe. She was content to listen to his heartbeat through the soft sweater against her cheek, but he tipped her chin up. His mouth brushed her forehead and he kissed her temple, spreading his hands across her back.

'Scarlett,' he muttered into her hair, 'look at me.'

Her lids fluttered up. His gaze was dark—the dark blue of the deep ocean—and what she saw in it made her catch her breath.

'Yes,' she said, putting a hand to his cheek. 'That's what I saw, and that's how I feel. I love you, Will. I never thought I'd be able to say those words to anyone again, but saying them to you is so easy.'

His mouth took hers then, in a kiss as deep and passionate as the ones which had haunted her dreams. He cupped her face in his hands to keep her steady, until he broke the contact and cradled her cheek against his chest.

'I've missed you so much. I've missed everything about you. Your smile and the joy of hearing you laugh, the feel of your hair through my fingers, your warmth, your scent. I promised myself if I ever got the chance I'd ask you what it is, so I need never be without a reminder of you.'

Scarlett smiled up at him. 'It's called Je Reviens. And I have come back.'

'If you'll give me your heart, I'll mend it so it's stronger than before and I'll take care of it for ever. Being without you has been unbearable, my love. I thought I'd lost you for ever, but now that you're back I don't ever want you to leave again.'

Scarlett reached up to touch his cheek. 'My heart belongs to you. I didn't know it until that night at the restaurant, but I'd already given it to you.'

Much later, Scarlett turned in his arms and rested her head on his chest. Will tucked her into his side, sliding his hand under the duvet and resting it on her stomach. Her skin quivered under his touch. He dropped a kiss onto her head.

Scarlett lifted her hand and raked her fingers across his chest, and he groaned.

'Please don't ever stop doing that. And please stay.'

'I intend to. Rozendal is my home.'

'I meant here, at Bellevale. All night. Every night. Always.'

'Isn't that breaking all the rules?'

'I love you.' He kissed her shoulder. 'And with you there are no rules because my love is unconditional. I don't want to be apart from you ever again. Will you marry me, Scarlett?'

Scarlett pushed herself upright and turned to look at him.

'Will…'

He pulled her down onto his chest, hooking a leg across her thigh, spearing his fingers into her hair. 'Please say yes.'

She bent her head. 'Yes,' she whispered into his mouth. 'Yes.'

* * * * *

If you enjoyed this story,
check out these other great reads from
Suzanne Merchant

Ballerina and the Greek Billionaire
Off-Limits Fling with the Billionaire
Their Wildest Safari Dream

All available now!